A FAMILY AFFAIR

A FAMILY AFFAIR

Alexander Ostrovsky

Adapted by Nick Dear

a b s o l u t e c l a s s i c s

First published in 1989 by Absolute Classics, an imprint of
Absolute Press, 14 Widcombe Crescent, Bath, England

Series Editor: Giles Croft

Cover and text design: Ian Middleton

Photoset by Quadraset Ltd, Midsomer Norton
Printed by WBC Print, Bristol
Bound by W. H. Ware & Son, Clevedon
Cover printed by Stopside Print, Bath

ISBN 0 948230 14 2

The first production of this version was toured by the Cheek By Jowl Theatre Company in the spring of 1988. It opened at the Donmar Warehouse Theatre on 27th April 1988, with the following cast:

BOLSHOV	Tam Dean Burn
AGRAFENA	Anne White
LIPOCHKA	Lesley Sharp
LAZAR	Adam Kotz
USTINYA	Marcia Warren
RISPOLOZHENSKY	Timothy Walker
FOMINISHNA	Annette Badland
TISHKA	Paul Stacey
DIRECTOR	Declan Donnellan
DESIGNER	Nick Ormerod
MUSIC DIRECTOR	Colin Sell
CHOREOGRAPHY	Anne Browne
LITERAL TRANSLATION	David Budgen

INTRODUCTION

Three things hit me when I started to work on *A Family Affair*. First, the vodka. Second, the shock as I realised how deceptive was its apparent simplicity. And third, a kind of unease as I began to feel that the only thing which had radically changed since the 1850s was that our tolerance of greed and dishonesty had probably increased.

Ostrovsky caused an uproar with this play, principally by suggesting that illegality was rife amongst the business classes, and that the judiciary connived in it. For us, that's an old story. 'Of course,' we say, 'we know it happens all the time.' So the balance of our interest in the storyline shifts. For example, the original contains far more detail about the merchant, Bolshov, and his insider-dealing schemes. Today's audience almost takes this for granted, and focuses instead on the upwardly-mobile young couple and their ostentatious ways.

In accentuating shifts of attention such as this, my version differs a little from the Russian. I have tried to make new jokes where the old ones weren't funny, and new plot where the old one chugged up a strange Muscovite siding of its own. I make no apology for this tactic; every dramatist must speak to their *own* generation, or they're dead.

For a first play, the complexity which lurks behind a simple storyline is quite astonishing. It's as if Ostrovsky had a kind of intuitive ability to make set-ups and pay-offs: the set-up in Act 1, the pay-off in Act 4 when you'd forgotten what the relevant strand of plot was in the first place. Perhaps it came naturally to him . . . or maybe he had to work hard like the rest of us.

NICK DEAR
JULY 1988

CHARACTERS

BOLSHOV	(Samson Silych Bolshov, a merchant)
AGRAFENA	(Agrafena Kondratyevna, his wife)
LIPOCHKA	(Olimpiada Samsonova, their daughter)
LAZAR	(Lazar Elizarich Podkhalyuzin, assistant to Bolshov)
USTINYA	(Ustinya Naumovna, a match-maker)
RISPOLOZHENSKY	(Sysoy Psoich Rispolozhensky, a solicitor)
FOMINISHNA	(A housekeeper)
TISHKA	(A boy)

ACT ONE

Bolshov's house.

LIPOCHKA: I love dancing. The new dances. I love them. There is
nothing in the world more exciting than going dancing.
You drive off to a do at the Assembly Rooms, say, or to
someone's wedding, you're simply dripping scent and
hothouse flowers, you're dressed up like a drawing in a
fashion magazine. Or a toy. A man's toy. You sit prettily.
You feign disinterest in the proceedings. Inside ten
seconds some young fellow's materialised at your
shoulder and he mutters, 'May I have the pleasure of this
dance?' The pleasure of this dance . . . If he looks as if he
can tell funny stories, or better still if he's an army man,
you lower your eyelids fractionally and reply, 'Why yes
you may.' Never take students, poets, or clerks. Stick
out for an army man. With a great big sword. And a
moustache. And epaulettes. And little tiny bells on his
spurs going tinkle-tinkle, tinkle-tinkle as he strides across
the room. Ooh . . . ! The sound of a young colonel as he
buckles on his sword! Like thunder crackling in my
heart. I want a military man. I don't want a pudding in
a dull civilian suit. I'd sooner die.

Most women at dances sit in the corners with their
doughy old legs crossed. Can't think why. It's such fun!
It's not difficult. At first I was a bit embarrassed in front
of my tutor – a Frenchman actually – but after twenty
lessons I understood everything perfectly. I learn quick.
The other girls don't, because they are dimwitted,
superstitious, and lacking the beneficiaries of a decent
education. My dancing-master touches my knees. Mama
gets horribly angry. But he has to do it. It's part of the
course.

(Strange faraway look.) I was just having a vision just
then. An officer in the Imperial Guard has proposed to
me. We are celebrating our engagement in the grand
style. Shimmering candles . . . waiters in white gloves . . .
My dress is made of tulle or gauze. A waltz strikes up. But

I decline to dance. My beau is disconcerted. I blush for shame. Perhaps he suspects that I am unschooled! He asks me what's the matter. What's the matter? What's the matter? *(Shrieks)* I haven't danced for a year and a half, that's what's the matter! I've forgotten the stupid steps!

She practises, waltzing badly. She's in her underwear.

LIPOCHKA: One, two three. One, two, three.

Enter Agrafena.

AGRAFENA: Caught you! In the act!

LIPOCHKA: I've got to practise!

AGRAFENA: Not before breakfast you haven't. You're shameless. Flouncing about like that in front of the window. And without even a bite of food inside you.

LIPOCHKA: Not true, Mama. I finished off the trifle and the last three cream meringues.

AGRAFENA: *(Following her around.)* What's wrong with eating bread and tea for breakfast like ordinary Christians? Will you stand still when I'm talking to you!

LIPOCHKA: Why should I? One, two, three –

AGRAFENA: Lipochka! Come here, you minx! Oh, this twirling and whirling and showing your legs, it's sinful!

LIPOCHKA: Not sinful. Everybody does it.

AGRAFENA: Stop. Or I'll bash your head against that table just as if I was a peasant threshing wheat.

Lipochka stops dancing and sits down.

LIPOCHKA: I'd finished anyway. Goodness, I'm perspiring like a horse. Give me your hankie, mummy.

AGRAFENA: I'll do it myself. *(Wipes Lipochka's brow.)* You've worn
yourself out, my angel. I expect you feel giddy, do you?
(Lipochka nods.) Sick? Feeling sick? *(She nods, rubbing
her tummy.)* Well don't say we never let you have your
own way.

LIPOCHKA: You ignorant old bag.

AGRAFENA: If you have no respect for me, at least have respect for the
walls of your father's house.

LIPOCHKA: All your ideas are completely out of date.

AGRAFENA: What a charming child you are. The way you treat your
mother . . . !

LIPOCHKA: You are repulsive. Like a corpse.

AGRAFENA: Have you nothing in your head but filth, miss? Did I
bring you into the world and suckle you at my own breast
and teach you everything you know to be compared in the
end to a dead person?

LIPOCHKA: You didn't teach me everything I know. Proper people
did. The truth is, mama, you never got educated at all.
You don't know a single thing. And when I popped out
of you, what was I fit for? I hadn't the first idea about life.
I behaved like a child. I couldn't dance. I didn't know
what cutlery to use for the fish course. I was a completely
pointless being. But when I got out on my own, I took a
look around at the world of taste and sensibility, and I
improved myself. And now I have to accept that I'm
vastly better equipped for life than most people. So why
should I listen to you?

AGRAFENA: One day you'll drive me mad.

LIPOCHKA: Only because you're a narrow-minded old bigot.

AGRAFENA: One day I shall throw myself to the ground in front of
your father and say, 'Samson Bolshov, that daughter of
ours is ruining my life.'

LIPOCHKA: Ruining *your* life? O ha ha. That's a good one. Very witty
             indeed.

AGRAFENA: Pardon?

LIPOCHKA: What about my life? What about the mess you've made
             of that? Why for instance did you send my last suitor
             packing? He was rather tasteful, he was. He was the best
             match I'm ever likely to make. Coming from a family like
             this. Well?

AGRAFENA: He had a filthy mouth.

LIPOCHKA: He never.

AGRAFENA: He swore!

LIPOCHKA: An oath of undying love. In French.

AGRAFENA: He minced around like a ballet dancer.

LIPOCHKA: He was a Grand Duke, mother! They walk like that!

AGRAFENA: Well I barely understood a word he spoke.

LIPOCHKA: He loved beauty. And style. And hunting bears. How
             dare you find fault with the higher things in life? He was
             a sight more refined than some scruffy merchant with a
             briefcase and inkstains on his cuff – ugh! *(Aside)* Boris,
             my love, my angel, take me, I'm yours.

AGRAFENA: You most certainly are not!

LIPOCHKA: You don't want me to be happy.

AGRAFENA: You're so stubborn, I sometimes wish I'd given you away
             to the village idiot. Yes! Fedot down the road! But you're
             probably too old now.

LIPOCHKA: Find me a real husband, mama . . . !

AGRAFENA: We're doing our best. Your father and me worry ourselves sick over it.

LIPOCHKA: The whole of Moscow to choose from – and they can't dig up one decent man.

AGRAFENA: They're not that thick on the ground to be honest.

LIPOCHKA: All my friends are married. Been married for years. I'm still hanging around. Look: find me a husband, and quick. Or else I'll take a lover.

AGRAFENA: No!

LIPOCHKA: Yes. I'll run off with a hussar. And marry him in secret.

AGRAFENA: You silly little slut. Hussars never have any money. I can see I'll have to call your father.

LIPOCHKA: Oh, the worst punishment – a conversation with father.

AGRAFENA: I may be simple, Lipochka, but I'm not daft. You know about as many hussars as I know archbishops. You've the devil in you, waggling your tongue. Little blue-eyes – why did you turn out like this? So naughty. So suspicious. And such a chubby baby. With such a turned-up nose. Put a stop to it, right now. Or you'll be down in the kitchen with your hands in the sink. I am your mother! – whilst I live. Lord have mercy on me. Any more cheek and you'll sleep with the pigs.

LIPOCHKA: That's right. You want to smother me in your own muck. You want to drive me to an early grave. And death is terribly unfashionable at the minute. – So I'm obnoxious. But what about you? You're absolutely vile! I'm your only daughter and you hate the sight of me. *(Coughs)* You wish I hadn't happened. All that rot about the devil! *(Coughs)* You'll kill me with your silly superstitions, you see my lungs are weak already – *(Starts to weep.)* Life is a fragile thing you know – *(Weeps)*

Agrafena stands and looks at her.

AGRAFENA: All right. That will do.

             Lipochka just weeps louder.

             There, there. Little baby . . . *(Lipochka weeps still.)*
             Stop, please stop . . . that's enough! Look I know it's my
             fault, I know we haven't done all we might, Lipochka,
             don't be cross with me . . . *(Agrafena starts to weep also.)*
             I'm only a stupid old woman, don't mind me . . .
             (They cry together.) Stop it, I'll buy you some earrings.

LIPOCHKA: Earrings? I've got a million earrings. I want emeralds.
             Buy me an emerald bracelet.

AGRAFENA: Anything you want, if you'll stop that wailing.

LIPOCHKA: The day I get married, I'll stop.

AGRAFENA: It will come soon, I promise. Kiss me. *(They kiss.)* God
             bless you. Come, let me dry your tears. All this talk about
             passing away, you're sounding like mad Fominishna.

LIPOCHKA: I'm warning you, mummy, if I don't get a husband soon
             I probably will turn out like her.

             Enter Fominishna.

FOMINISHNA: Agrafena, my dear – guess who's come to visit?

AGRAFENA: How do I know, I'm not clairvoyant.

LIPOCHKA: Why don't you ask me? You're perfectly well aware that
             I'm cleverer than the pair of you put together.

FOMINISHNA: You're quick. Your brain's as sharp as mustard, I
             admit. But it's all mouth, isn't it? It's all chat, and very
             little action. Specially when it comes to being civil to your
             friends.

AGRAFENA: Exactly so, Fominishna.

FOMINISHNA: A drop more generosity wouldn't go amiss, Lipochka.

LIPOCHKA: Pathetic old fool. Had a bottle of stout for breakfast by the sound of it.

FOMINISHNA: And what if I did? Life is short. One day you die and that's the end of everything. I don't want to get there and drift away sadly down a river of regret. In my philosophy you drink beer for breakfast if you feel like it.

AGRAFENA: I can't follow a word you say. My ears drop off with your talking. Who is it who's at the door?

LIPOCHKA: A woman or a man?

FOMINISHNA: You've got men on the brain! When did you last see a man wearing a bonnet, and widow's weeds?

AGRAFENA: It's a woman then.

LIPOCHKA: Of course it is. But who?

FOMINISHNA: You're the great genius. You tell me.

LIPOCHKA: Don't muck around, you imbecile!

FOMINISHNA: It's Ustinya Naumovna.

USTINYA: *(Off)* And next time, pull your finger out!

FOMINISHNA: She's just in the middle of an argument with the yardboy concerning the precise speed with which he opened the gate. She'll be up any second.

LIPOCHKA: At last . . .

USTINYA: *(Approaching)* Those stairs are bloody steep. It's like climbing a mountain.

    Enter Ustinya.

    My dears, how do you do . . .

LIPOCHKA: It's wonderful to see you, Ustinya.

USTINYA: Wait your turn, young lady.

                Ustinya and Agrafena kiss formally.

                Agrafena, my dear.

AGRAFENA: Dear Ustinya, welcome.

USTINYA: Survived another bitter night, it would appear?

AGRAFENA: As you see, I'm still alive and kicking. Thanks be to God.

ALL: Amen.

AGRAFENA: Life is good to me. There is plenty to eat these days. And
                I have a darling daughter. Do you know, Ustinya, we've
                just spent the whole morning together, laughing and
                joking and carrying on.

USTINYA: She must be after something. A new frock I expect.
                (Kisses Lipochka.) I say, putting on weight, Lipochka?

LIPOCHKA: No I am not. I'm losing weight actually. It's all the worry
                about my future. I get pains in my stomach, my heart
                hammers in my breast, some days I feel myself going
                down, down, as if I were being sucked to the bottom of
                the sea.

AGRAFENA: Oh dear.

LIPOCHKA: I'm quite faint with melancholy . . .

USTINYA: Fominishna, a quick kiss from you. *(They kiss. To
                Agrafena.)* We've already met outside. The poor dear's
                been blinding me with all the very latest new theories . . .

FOMINISHNA: I'm only common people, I know. Country people. But
                we've got brains too. We're entitled to hold an opinion.

                The others laugh at her. Agrafena sits down.

AGRAFENA: Sit down, Ustinya, sit down. We don't act too formal in

this house. I hope you mayn't mind. Fominishna, run
and tell them to warm up the samovar.

USTINYA: I've had my tea. I shouldn't think I shall want any more
tea for quite some time.

AGRAFENA: Fominishna, old girl, are you awake?

LIPOCHKA: Her mind's wandering. I'll go, mummy. You know what
a slug she is.

FOMINISHNA: I am perfectly capable of doing my job, thank you. I was
wondering, dear Agrafena, if it might perhaps be nicer
to serve some cherry vodka and salt-fish, to such an
auspicious guest? Rather than the samovar?

AGRAFENA: I think we should have – both. We can afford it.

FOMINISHNA: As you wish, ma'am. *(Exit)*

AGRAFENA: . . . Do you have any news for us, Ustinya? My little girl
is on tenterhooks.

LIPOCHKA: You're round here every day. But nothing ever happens.

USTINYA: That's because you're not exactly the easiest family in the
world to satisfy. It all takes time. Your father yearns for a
wealthy man. Fedot, the nutter down the road, would
suffice if only he was rolling in money. He has all the
other attributes, apparently. It's a question of how big a
dowry must be paid. Your mother desires a life of simple
and unassuming luxury and for her a merchant is the only
answer. But not just any old merchant. No, he's got to be
a Guild man, from one of the top five ranks. And he must
drive the best horses. And he must say prayers before
bed. And presumably you have several frightfully modern
ideas of your own. How is one to please everybody? One
would have to create a man from scratch!

AGRAFENA: *(Crosses herself.)* Ustinya, please!

          *Fominishna enters and places vodka and snacks on the
          table.*

LIPOCHKA: I'll never marry a merchant, never! I wasn't brought up
              for that. I speak French! Play the piano! Dance like a
              butterfly! I don't care where you get him, I want a
              nobleman.

AGRAFENA: *(To Ustinya.)* See? *(To Fominishna.)* You try talking to
              her.

FOMINISHNA: Where on earth do you pick up these ideas about the
              aristocracy? What do you see in them? They're shiftless,
              idle good-for-nothings the lot of them. They're not clean
              you know. Have you ever seen one at the bath-house?
              And they shave their faces! Their flabby chops all naked
              to the world. It's utterly unhygienic.

LIPOCHKA: What do you know about it? You were born a peasant,
              and you'll still have pig-dirt between your toes when they
              lay you in your grave. What use is a merchant to me?
              What standing has he in society? What pride in himself?
              You think I should be attracted by his filthy beard?

AGRAFENA: It is not a filthy beard, but the hairs that belongeth to our
              Lord. And He has numbered them. And He does not
              want them scraped and hacked away. You kiss your
              father. He's got a beard.

LIPOCHKA: Kissing daddy is one thing. Kissing my *lover* is another.

AGRAFENA: Oh! You'll wash your mouth out with soap for that.

LIPOCHKA: I thought I had made myself perfectly clear: no
              businessmen. At the very, very least: a Count. If not, I'll
              cry from now till the day I die. If I run out of tears I'll eat
              pepper.

FOMINISHNA: Oh, heavens, you're not going to start crying? I beg you,
              no. Life's too short. Have you upset your daughter,
              Agrafena?

AGRAFENA: No! She's always been like this. She'd never eat what she
              was given.

USTINYA: Well, if it's the food she craves, I'll find her a nice, tasty
              nobleman, shall I?

LIPOCHKA: Oh yes please!

USTINYA: What sort do you prefer? Thick and beefy or long and
              lean?

LIPOCHKA: I don't care! I've nothing against him being bigger than
              the average. But he mustn't be too small. Of course I'd
              prefer a nicely filled-out one with good posture to some
              droopy little fellow. Dark hair if possible. Or fair if you
              like. But if he's not dressed like the chap on page seven
              of last month's magazine, you can forget it. Has my hair
              turned to rats'-tails, it feels like it has . . . ?

USTINYA: I have a husband for you.

LIPOCHKA: Fetch me the combs, Fominish – what?

USTINYA: A nobleman. Tall. Virile.

LIPOCHKA: A miracle! Did you hear, mama?

AGRAFENA: Has he peasants?

USTINYA: He has. Lipochka, off you go and tidy yourself up whilst
              I have a few words with your mother.

LIPOCHKA: Come and visit me in my room, soon as you can – I shall
              want to know all his personal details.

                         Lipochka and Fominishna exit.

AGRAFENA: . . . Perhaps a little tot before the tea arrives?

USTINYA: A medicinal vodka? To take the sting off the air?

AGRAFENA: *(Pours)* Quite.

USTINYA: How agreeable.

AGRAFENA:	Your very good health.
USTINYA:	A very long life. *(Drinks)* Aargh! Where did you get this poison?
AGRAFENA:	At the wine shop.
USTINYA:	Do you buy it by the bucket?
AGRAFENA:	Yes. A bottle's never enough to go round. Our living costs are – well, no expense spared, I can tell you.
USTINYA:	*(With an incredulous look.)* I know, the price of things when one has to pay for them oneself . . . ! It makes me shiver. I've been working my fingers to the bone all winter on your behalf, Agrafena. I've slogged up and down the best streets and in and out of some of the finest houses in the land – to which, fortunately, my status gives me access – in order to find you an eligible man. Listen, I don't exaggerate – noble blood, private means, not very ugly. I'm rather good at this work, don't you think?
AGRAFENA:	I am sure that my husband will see you well rewarded.
USTINYA:	Out of courtesy, I shall accept. But what a man I've bagged! Plenty of peasants, imperial orders dangling round his neck, likeable and surprisingly intelligent.
AGRAFENA:	Then you had better warn him that our daughter does not have – how to phrase it delicately? – dirty great piles of gold.
USTINYA:	He's got so much of his own, he'll never notice.
AGRAFENA:	Good. Good! Only one thing, Ustinya. I've never had an aristocrat for a son-in-law before. I don't know how you behave. What do you say to them? I'll be struck dumb. I'll be lost in a forest of embarrassment.
USTINYA:	Yes, it'll be strange for you both at first. But the quality are extremely tolerant people. He'll make allowances, I'm sure.

Enter Rispolozhensky.

RISPOLO: Hello? May I come in? Why, Madame Bolshov, how marvellous to see you. I was hoping to discuss a legal matter with your husband, but apparently he is otherwise engaged. So I thought, I know, I'll go and see – that's not cherry vodka on the table, is it? At this time of morning? Oh, go on then, tempt me. Just a tiny drop.

AGRAFENA: Help yourself, Rispolozhensky. Sit down. You're welcome.

RISPOLO: *(Drinks)* Cheerio. First of the day.

AGRAFENA: How is everything with you?

RISPOLO: A dog's life, Mme. Bolshov, a dog's life. Spend most of it waiting around for business meetings. I'm wasting away, I am. You know what it's like: big family, small profit. Oh, I'm wasting away, for sure. Thankfully I don't grumble. I'm not the grumbling sort.

AGRAFENA: It's a sin to grumble at the good Lord's designs.

RISPOLO: It is indeed.

USTINYA: Amen.

RISPOLO: Did I ever tell you the story of the man who moans and moans and –

USTINYA: What's your name again?

RISPOLO: Rispolozhensky.

USTINYA: Oh. Well, I've heard worse.

AGRAFENA: You haven't told that story, no.

RISPOLO: It's a true one. There's not a lie in it. Might I just –

AGRAFENA: Please, please. We don't stint in this house.

RISPOLO: *(Pours, drinks.)* Very decent of you. Well – first of the day. Once upon a time a very old man lived in the province of . . . hell, I've forgotten where exactly . . . some place or other, uninhabited I think. This old boy had twelve daughters and the amazing thing is that every one of them was slightly younger than the one before. When he got old he unforeseeably got too weak to work. Oddly enough his wife was old also, whereas the children on the other hand were young. Still, you have to look out for them, don't you? Now, our friends had gone through everything they had by the time they came to this predicament. There wasn't a crumb in the house. 'I know,' thought the old man. 'I'll go and sit by the crossroads and hold out my hand, and surely the kind citizens of this district will take pity.' He sat the whole of one day. 'Have faith,' said the passers-by, 'God will provide.' He sat the whole of the second day: ditto. At the end of the third day he did the unforgiveable –

AGRAFENA: He didn't!

RISPOLO: He did. He began to grumble.

AGRAFENA: Oh, my word!

RISPOLO: 'Dear Christ in heaven,' he called out. 'I'm no cheat, no bribe-taker, no extortionist – and yet I cannot get enough to live. Better to kill myself, than this!'

AGRAFENA: The fool!

USTINYA: What a terrible story.

AGRAFENA: He sounds as bad as my husband!

Bolshov approaches, grumbling.

RISPOLO: And that night, ladies, in a dream, he –

Enter Bolshov.

BOLSHOV: Oh, you're here, are you? What's the sermon today then?

USTINYA: Good morning, Samson Bolshov.

RISPOLO: *(Bowing)* I trust I find you in good health, sir.

BOLSHOV: *(Sits, delicately.)* My piles are giving me gyp.

AGRAFENA: So what happened to the old man *then?*

RISPOLO: Dear Mme. Bolshov, one evening when our time is our
                own, I'll come by and tell you the moral of the story.

BOLSHOV: Taking up morality, are you, wife? Is that wise for
                someone with such a miniscule brain?

AGRAFENA: That's just like you. You cannot cope with the thought of
                people having a genuine, serious, heart-to-heart talk.

BOLSHOV: I've an idea for a heart-to-heart talk, ask
                Mr. Rispolozhensky about the file he took from the
                magistrates court and then – *(Chuckles)* and then lost in a
                bar, there's a genuine, serious subject for a heart-to-heart
                talk.

RISPOLO: I didn't lose it in a bar. That's a very far cry from the
                truth.

BOLSHOV: What did happen, then?

RISPOLO: It was a misunderstanding! Let me explain,
                Mme. Bolshov. I took a confidential file out of the court
                because a solicitor's clerk often has to study the evidence
                for the next day's hearing. On the way to my lodgings I
                bumped into a very old friend from way back – you know
                what it's like. You have to have a drink or two so as not to
                seem unfriendly. He led me into a bar. And in the natural
                course of events I seem to have, well, forgive me, ended
                up marginally paralytic, it could happen to anyone.

AGRAFENA: Of course it could.

RISPOLO: It's the price you pay for your sociability. Somehow or
                other I returned home, I don't recall by what route

exactly. And the next day went to work quite unruffled by
the experience. And we needed the file. And it wasn't
there. A fearful commotion. The clerk of the court
helped me to search my rooms. Twice. They were about
to press charges when I suddenly remembered – the
boyhood friend! The seedy bar! I set off at once with the
clerk and two or three other uniformed officials and we
found the document immediately via the barmaid and I
was set free with the court's thanks!

BOLSHOV: The only flaw in that story is the fact that they gave you
the sack.

RISPOLO: An oversight on my part.

BOLSHOV: Personally I'm surprised they didn't send you to Siberia.

RISPOLO: Why would they want to send me to Siberia?

BOLSHOV: Because you're a disgrace to your profession,
Rispolozhensky, that's why. Because you're a
dipsomaniac.

AGRAFENA: What's that?

USTINYA: A drunk.

AGRAFENA: Oh.

RISPOLO: They make allowances for that. When I heard they
wanted to put me on trial for misconduct I ran straight to
the General who runs my department and I threw myself
at his feet, Mme. Bolshov, that's what I did, I ate the dirt
on his riding boot and I said, 'Your Excellency, I have
five children. And a wife. Don't let me be ruined for ever.'
He said, 'I don't kick a man when he's down. Just hand
in your notice and never show your face here again and
that'll be the end of it.' Yes! He pardoned me! 'God bless
you, sir,' I cried, 'God bless you!' And now on every holy
day I take him cakes and wine. Which reminds me . . .

AGRAFENA: Please, you go ahead.

RISPOLO: Well, if you twist my arm. *(Pours a drink.)* First of the day, Mr. Bolshov.

AGRAFENA: Ustinya, come with me and see if the samovar's ready. Also I've got a marvellous little something to add to Lipochka's bottom drawer . . .

USTINYA: You do have a quite extraordinary amount laid by for her.

AGRAFENA: Well you see dear the new fabrics have just come out. And it's not as if we have to pay real money for them, is it?

USTINYA: Since you have your own shop, no, I don't suppose you do.

Exit Agrafena and Ustinya.

BOLSHOV: So, Mr. Rispolozhensky.

RISPOLO: Sir.

BOLSHOV: No doubt an ocean of ink will drip from your pen in pursuit of this dirty old business.

RISPOLO: *(Laughs)* The ink will cost you nothing. I just wondered whether you'd come to any conclusions about your situation . . . ?

BOLSHOV: Oh, you just wondered? How charitable. Frankly, I am of the opinion that you are a lot of vultures. Sniff of blood on the wind and down you swoop.

RISPOLO: Me swoop? Sir, I would not know how to begin to swoop. I simply want to help you out . . . But you know your own affairs.

BOLSHOV: Hardly any better than you do, you vulture. Your scrawny neck craned into every transaction. Christ, we tradespeople are such fools to put our trust in you! You'll pick clean our bones before you're done.

RISPOLO: That is a completely unimaginable hypothesis, sir. I am not a beast. I would never desecrate your remains, on that you may depend for as long as you live. I hold you in the warmest regard, Mr. Bolshov.

BOLSHOV: Sure, sure, you love us, lawyers love merchants like leeches love blood. I am sick with worry over all this. I long to be shot of it, once and for all.

RISPOLO: You're not the first to do it, Mr. Bolshov, and you won't be the last.

BOLSHOV: Damn right, and if they get away with it, why shouldn't I? And the extent to which they do get away with it . . . ! Shameful. Riding around in fancy carriages, buying mansions in town, pavilions in the country, furniture so posh they daren't sit in it, living up to their eyeballs in debt until one sunny day they announce they've gone bust. Then try getting anything out of them. The carriages disappear Christ knows where. The houses have been mortgaged and the creditors can think themselves lucky if they come away with two or three pairs of old boots. And that's the end of it. They'll swindle the shirt off a poor trader's back! They'll leave him destitute, wandering in some fiscal wilderness. *My* creditors on the other hand are rich men to begin with. I wouldn't be doing them any real damage.

RISPOLO: Indeed not.

BOLSHOV: Are you certain you can handle this? I mean have you got the balls, Rispolozhensky, have you got the nerve to see it through? How do I know you won't lose me everything?

RISPOLO: My dear sir, I am hardly a virgin in these matters. I've spread my legs for half the town, in a legal manner of speaking. And got away with it, too. Anyone else would have been shipped to Siberia by now. If I might just top up my supplies . . . ? *(Pours, drinks.)* The first thing you've got to do is transfer the ownership of your house and your shops.

BOLSHOV: Agreed.

RISPOLO: But only on paper, of course.

BOLSHOV: Of course. Purely temporary measure.

RISPOLO: This must be done as soon as possible.

BOLSHOV: Agreed. Who shall we dump them on? *(They consider.)* What about the wife?

RISPOLO: No, I'm afraid that's against the law.

BOLSHOV: I thought the whole thing was against the law.

RISPOLO: Ah, no, it isn't, actually. If we observe the minutiae we will find ourselves protected by the law. And anyone looking for trouble will walk smack into a wall of technical jargon, all perfectly legitimate and completely impenetrable. But you can't transfer your property to your wife, it's not valid in court. Let's do the thing correctly. You must be seen to hand over the deeds to an outsider.

BOLSHOV: The problem with that is he might get attached to them. Unshakeably. Like a tapeworm in the belly of a cow.

RISPOLO: Then you have to make sure you get someone with a conscience. Someone who understands what a gentleman's agreement is.

BOLSHOV: And where do you propose, in these times, I find one of them? Everyone I know would stick a knife in my gut if I glanced in the other direction.

RISPOLO: I have a suggestion. Listen to me or don't listen to me, as you wish.

BOLSHOV: I'm listening.

RISPOLO: What kind of man is your assistant?

BOLSHOV: Who? Lazar?

RISPOLO: Yes. That one. Lazar . . . Elizarich, is it?

BOLSHOV: Hmm . . . Lazar, you think? . . . Well, he's a bright lad,
            works hard . . . Apparently he's already got a little
            money of his own. Which should reduce the temptation.
            So . . . Lazar. Let it be him.

RISPOLO: Then shall I draw up a deed of transfer, Mr. Bolshov, to
            assign all your property to his name?

BOLSHOV: Yes. But you make bloody sure it comes back. If you get
            me through this cleanly, my friend, I will see you're very
            well looked after. Very well looked after indeed.

RISPOLO: I'll drink to that. Will you speak to Lazar concerning this
            matter?

BOLSHOV: I've got a meeting with him shortly. He's sensible. He
            knows the meaning of a nod and a wink. Once I've
            transferred the house to him, what do I do?

RISPOLO: We'll draw up a proposal which we'll send to all those
            who claim you owe them money. It says, this is the
            situation, down on my luck, have had to mortgage
            myself, as witness this paperwork et cetera et cetera.
            Appertaining to the outstanding debt I am able to offer
            you repayment of one quarter, ie., twenty-five kopecks
            on each rouble owing, which, am sure you'll agree,
            considerably better than nothing. – And then you'll do
            the rounds. If anyone squawks, you up it a little, or if
            they really turn vicious, pay back in full, but not before
            they sign a receipt saying they have only accepted twenty-
            five kopecks on each rouble. This you can show to the
            others, viz, here it is in black and white, so-and-so's
            agreed to my terms, fail to understand your hesitation.

BOLSHOV: Splendid. No harm in negotiating, is there? If they piss
            on twenty-five they'll take fifty. If half a rouble's still not
            enough, they'll surely snatch at seventy kopecks. It's an
            improvement on bugger-all. My daughter's ready to be
            married. Christ knows who'll take her. But she is a non-
            earning investment, Rispolozhensky, and it's time she

was off my hands. So I need to get myself sorted. We
could all do with a decent rest, couldn't we? Get our feet
up, let business go to hell.

Enter Lazar.

Ah, Lazar, just the man. Straight up from town? How's it
all coming along?

LAZAR: The wheels are turning, sir, thank heaven. Morning,
             Mr. Rispolozhensky.

RISPOLO: *(Bows)* Good day to you, Lazar Elizarich.

BOLSHOV: I am glad to hear there is a motion of some kind, Lazar,
             but unfortunately it is not translating itself into profit. We
             sell and sell, but what we make on our turnover is barely
             worth getting up in the morning for. Are the shop-boys to
             blame? Are they slipping stuff out for their girlfriends,
             grandmas, God knows who? Appeal to their sense of
             loyalty. Don't they know the bloody business by now?

LAZAR: Incontrovertibly they do, sir. I speak to them regular.

BOLSHOV: What do you say?

LAZAR: The normal sort of things, sir. 'Wake up, lads,' I say.
             'The owner, Samson Bolshov, is depending on you. Keep
             your eyes peeled for customers with more money than
             sense. Try and shift last year's fashions. The shop-soiled
             stock. The slightly-imperfect under-the-counter junk.
             Always some berk who will buy it. Always some fat
             debutante who will fail to notice a slight increase in the
             price of silk.'

BOLSHOV: It's a matter of technique.

LAZAR: Dead right it is. 'And you can measure your cloth a little
             more, um, instinctively,' I tell them. 'Stretch it till it's
             ready to split. Lord have mercy on us for what we do.
             But we don't have to wear the stuff, do we?'

Rispolozhensky laughs.

BOLSHOV: Excellent. After all the wholesale tailors rob us blind to begin with. It's the same the whole world over.

RISPOLO: It certainly is. Those tailors – phaw! Villains.

BOLSHOV: They're scum. And we're at the sharp end, because it's us as has to deal with the public. Lazar, my boy, profit's not what it used to be, Jesus no. *(Significant pause.)* Don't suppose you've got a newspaper, have you?

LAZAR: By all means, Mr. Bolshov.

Lazar takes the paper from his pocket and gives it to Bolshov.

BOLSHOV: Let's have a quick look. *(Puts on his reading glasses.)*

RISPOLO: I'll need a small drink if I'm reading. *(Drinks, then puts on glasses and reads over Bolshov's shoulder.)*

BOLSHOV: *(Reading)* Government and Miscellaneous Societies' Notices . . . *(Reads on.)* Well damn me. Here, just listen to this, Lazar! On the twenty-first day of September and according to the verdict of the Court of Commerce, the merchant Selivestrov Pleshkov of the First Guild was declared insolvent. Hah! Look! There's a big shot Selivestrov for you! He's gone up in smoke! Tell me, Lazar – does he owe us for anything?

LAZAR: He owes us for sugar, sir. Three hundred sacks.

BOLSHOV: That's bad. That's bad. Still, not to worry, I'm sure he'll pay me back in full, out of friendliness.

LAZAR: I have my doubts about that, sir.

BOLSHOV: We'll settle it between ourselves, anyhow. *(Reads)* Moscow Merchant of the First Guild Antip Sysoev Yenotov was declared insolvent. – The pious one. What about him?

LAZAR: He owes us for cooking oil, sir.

BOLSHOV: Does he by God! These bastards will cross themselves with one hand and pick your pocket with the other! Don't trust any of them. Here's a third bankrupt: Moscow Merchant of the Second Guild Efrem Lakin Poluarshinnikov was today declared insolvent.

LAZAR: We've got a credit note from that one.

BOLSHOV: Is it valid?

LAZAR: Yes, but he's gone into hiding.

BOLSHOV: And another: Samopalov. I don't believe this, do you, Lazar? Four bankrupts in a day? Yesterday all one hundred per cent solvent? Bollocks. I suspect they are plotting together. Some kind of scheme to escape from their debts.

LAZAR: All a lot of rascals, sir.

BOLSHOV: I think an inside-man is setting up the deals. Take the rag away.

LAZAR: The names soil the paper they're printed on, sir.

Significant pause. They stare at him.

RISPOLO: I must get off home, Mr. Bolshov. I have some writing to do.

BOLSHOV: Stay.

RISPOLO: No, I'll leave you gentlemen to talk commerce. I'll look in tomorrow. Good day. Good day, Lazar.

Exit Rispolozhensky.

BOLSHOV: . . . You fancy yourself as a businessman, don't you? And I suspect you think money slips into our coffers like the melting snow off the roof. But let me ask you something – is it real money? Is it actual cash you can spend? 'What do you mean, pay cash?' the customer will say. 'What a

preposterous idea. Who carries cash nowadays? I insist
you accept my promissory note.' So you must. 'Cash!
Hah!' So you end up like me with a hundred thousand
roubles' worth of useless credit notes, heaped around the
house like old love letters. I'll sell you the whole damn lot
for half a rouble. But just try finding the signatory. You
can roam the streets of Moscow with a pack of baying
dogs, you will still never corner your debtors. Am I right
or am I wrong?

LAZAR: Dead right, sir.

BOLSHOV: Nothing but credit notes. Pieces of paper. If you trade
them on discount, the percentage you'll get is so low it'll
give you ulcers. I've got ulcers. They're not very nice.
Look, Lazar, I have a candle business, a fancy-goods
shop, and a grocery chain, but not one of them is
bringing me luck, do you get my drift?

LAZAR: . . . Yes, I believe I do.

BOLSHOV: Then how do you think I should proceed?

LAZAR: I am not paid to think. I am paid to carry out your orders.

BOLSHOV: Well, I'm not giving orders. I'm asking, very cordially,
your opinion.

            Pause

            Lazar.

LAZAR: Sir?

BOLSHOV: Are you . . . fond of me? *(Pause)* An honest answer,
please. *(Pause)* Yes or no? Why don't you speak? *(Pause)*
Haven't I fed and watered you, put a roof over your head,
Christ, set you up in the world?

LAZAR: Samson Bolshov – I am offended that you need to ask.
You must not doubt my affection for yourself and your
family. All I can say is, count me in.

BOLSHOV: . . . Count you in to what exactly?

LAZAR: Whatever you require. I will not let you down.

BOLSHOV: No need to say any more, Lazar. We understand each other. Now is the time to move. Today. Payment is due on all my notes. Why wait? Hang around, and some little wank who owes *me* money will show up and skin us alive. He'll make a deal at ten kopecks per rouble and then sit tight on his fortune like a fat frog on a rock, while we, the honest tradesmen, blame our own incompetence for our downfall, and scrabble around for salvation . . . I think I'll say I've gone bust and offer my creditors twenty-five kopecks on each rouble. I have just enough ready cash. Will they bite? What do you reckon?

LAZAR: The way I see it – if you're only offering twenty-five kopecks, you might as well offer nothing at all. It's more honest.

BOLSHOV: . . . I think I take your meaning. We'll screw them as hard as we can! I am transferring, for the interim, the ownership of my house and shops to you. Christ, I do get anxious about all this . . . !

LAZAR: Occupational hazard, isn't it? – I recommend we then ship all our stock as far off as possible, the Baltic coast perhaps?

BOLSHOV: I'm getting old, Lazar. I'll stake everything on this last game. If you're with me.

LAZAR: I'm with you, sir. Through all the fires of hell. *(They shake hands.)*

BOLSHOV: Good boy! Why should a man like me spend his last days on earth scratching around for kopecks? One big play, and I'm out of the woods. Free and clear. *(Embraces Lazar.)* Thanks, Lazar. Stand by me now, and we'll split whatever we make – I'll give you two and a half per cent, how's that?

LAZAR: All I ask is to see you at peace with yourself, Mr. Bolshov.
            I've lived with you practically all my life. I know what a
            good man you are. Why, I came to you as a snot-nosed
            kid, off the frozen streets, I had no home, no family, yet
            you took me in and treated me as one of your own, do you
            remember?

            Exit Bolshov, reminiscing happily.

            And within a short time you had me sweeping your yard,
            cleaning your chimneys, and mucking out your pigs.
            (With a smile.) And I am deeply grateful.

                    END OF ACT ONE

ACT TWO

Bolshov's house.

TISHKA: *(With a large broom.)* Call this a life? Get up and sweep the entire house before daybreak? Me? This family are eccentric. I'm telling you. If any other boss employs a lad, this lad lives with the rest of the lads – you're in the shop all day, you get a little time to yourself. Here it's do this, do that, come in, get out, I'm running through the town like a lunatic. 'Don't complain,' they say, 'you're lucky to be learning a trade.' Oh yeah. Very likely.

Respectable people keep a yardman for odd jobs. We've a yardman here, too. Round about now he'll be lying by the stove with the kittens. Or shafting the cook in the pantry. So I'm the one who gets picked on. In respectable peoples' homes the atmosphere's a bit more relaxed, like they're not trying to prove nothing. Get in a spot of trouble, they say, 'It's all right, he's young.' Here, you're held to account for bleeding everything. If it's not the old man it's his Mrs. She can't half dish it out. Or it's that creepy clerk Lazar. Or dippy Fominishna. The place is full of low-lifes, pushing me around. It is absolutely disgusting and intolerable. It's driving me crackers!

Hits the furniture with his broom.

I'm going funny in the brains!

Hits the furniture and the walls. Lazar has come in and is watching him.

LAZAR: What are you up to, runt?

TISHKA: I'm dusting!

LAZAR: Dusting? You're up to a lot of fucking mischief, aren't you? I'm going to knock your teeth so far down your throat you'll have to stick that brush up your arse to clean them.

TISHKA: I'll speak to the boss!

LAZAR: Speak to the boss? What, old Bolshov? You think he frightens me? As far as you're concerned, runt, I'm the boss. You need a good hiding to keep you on the straight and narrow, don't you? Think of it as further education. I got the same treatment myself, and it never did me any harm.

TISHKA: No, you turned out a model human being.

LAZAR: Right, kid. *(Goes to hit him.)*

TISHKA: Just try it, Lazar! I'll tell on you! Honest to God!

LAZAR: *(Releases him)* Give me some information and I'll spare your life. Has Rispolozhensky been here?

TISHKA: Course he has. Loads of times.

LAZAR: I mean today, Tishka!

TISHKA: Course you do.

LAZAR: Did he say he might look in again?

TISHKA: Course he did.

LAZAR: All right. You can go.

TISHKA: If the lawyer's coming – won't you want some rowanberry vodka?

LAZAR: Vodka . . . good idea. *(Gives Tishka money.)* Buy half a bottle, and get yourself a cake with the change. But be quick, I don't want you missed around here.

TISHKA: I'll be as quick as a flash, Lazar. *(Exit)*

LAZAR: . . . It's a total disaster, it blinds me like a fog. I don't know what the bleeding hell to do! The creditors called his bluff! Twenty-five kopecks got laughed at! So now

he's going to have to declare himself formally bankrupt.
Prison. Courts of Commerce. Business goes to the wall.
How will I survive? Selling shit up a back-street? I've
sweated blood for them for twenty years, now they just
let me go under? Like fuck!

Maybe I could sell his merchandise. Might find a buyer
on the Baltic. But wait. They say a man must listen to his
conscience. Well indubitably he must. However let's put
it in perspective. If you're dealing with a good bloke, of
course you pay attention to your conscience. On the other
hand, what if you're dealing with a swindler? Samson
Bolshov is one of the richest merchants in holy Russia.
All this is just a fiddle he's contrived for his own benefit.
Me, I'm a working man. Why should I care what happens
to someone who is, technically, a criminal?

I'm daydreaming again. Little Lipochka, or – what's her
formal name, no-one here ever uses it – Olimpiada – she's
a very highly educated young woman, you know. She's
more unique than most. But no posh suitor will take her
without no bloody dowry! They'll have to settle her on a
merchant. I've got prospects. Why shouldn't I go to
Bolshov and say, 'Sir, there comes a time in a young
man's life when he starts to think about the furtherance
of the line. Sir, your daughter – Miss Olimpiada – is a
sophisticated lady, but as you can see, I am not exactly a
yokel. Besides, I have some savings. I am respectful to my
elders. Why don't you give her to me?'

    Tishka returns.

If that doesn't work, I can always remind the old sod that
I hold the deeds to his house and his shops . . . It's
amazing how that can move a man to a quick decision.
(Sees Tishka.)

TISHKA: I just got back!

LAZAR: Listen, Tishka – is Ustinya Naumovna here?

TISHKA: She's upstairs. The solicitor's on his way, too.

LAZAR: Good. Set out the vodka, and clear off.

             Tishka puts vodka and glasses on the table, and exits.

             If I make a good case for myself . . . a good, slick
             presentation . . . I'll be walking up the aisle in a week.
             Fantastic! It's all starting to go my way! I feel like
             climbing up the bell-tower of Ivan the Great!

             Enter Rispolozhensky.

             Good day to you, sir.

RISPOLO: The same to you, dear Lazar. Are my eyes deceiving me
             or is there a scent of rowanberry in the air? I wouldn't say
             no to a taste, Lazar. – Something dreadful's happened.

LAZAR: *(In panic.)* What?

RISPOLO: My hands have started trembling in the mornings.
             Especially this one, which I write with. Also this one a
             little bit. In order to write anything at all I have to try and
             hold this one steady with this one. Alternatively a small
             glass of vodka does the trick.

LAZAR: Why do your hands shake?

RISPOLO: From worry, I expect. I've a wife and five little ones.
             They all have to be fed or they die you know. First one
             needs a school uniform. Then another needs medicine.
             The third wants – and my house is miles out of town! I
             wear out a pair of boots a week just walking in to the
             business quarter. And why do I bother? There are days
             when I don't take home even half a rouble! What are
             you supposed to live on? Vodka? *(This reminds him.
             He drinks.)* So I thought, I know, I'll drop in on Lazar
             Elizarich, perhaps he can help me out with some cash.

LAZAR: What sort of fiddle is it for?

RISPOLO: Fiddle? What do you mean, fiddle? That's not a nice
             word to use, Lazar, not a nice word at all! Come on, man.

Haven't I served you well? I went to a lot of trouble to
suggest you to Bolshov as a suitable 'outsider' – and to
draw up the deed of transfer, too.

LAZAR: You've already been paid for that. And watch your
tongue! They listen at keyholes in this house.

RISPOLO: Quite correct, I have been paid, perfectly correct, Lazar,
yes. But I am sunk so low in poverty. It barely scratched
the surface of my debts.

LAZAR: I know poverty. *(Pause. Then he lays his wallet on the
table.)* Actually, I'm carrying a load of spare cash around
at the moment, Rispolozhensky, and it's spoiling the line
of my suit.

RISPOLO: Spare cash? – Are you pulling my leg?

LAZAR: No.

RISPOLO: If you're flush, could you help me out? You'll get your
reward in heaven.

LAZAR: Will I? Do you need a lot?

RISPOLO: Three roubles?

LAZAR: Why so little?

RISPOLO: Give me five, then.

LAZAR: Wallet's bulging. You should ask for more.

RISPOLO: You're very kind. I'll take ten.

LAZAR: Ten roubles! That *is* a lot. For nothing.

RISPOLO: It's not for nothing! I've earned it! I'm taking a very big
risk.

LAZAR: How much did Bolshov promise you for dealing with this
business?

RISPOLO: I'm ashamed to say I accepted the brief for a thousand
            roubles and a second-hand racoon-skin coat. Nobody in
            Moscow works for less than me.

LAZAR: I'll give you two thousand. For this same job that you
            have already done. And for keeping your trap shut about
            it. But I want you to make sure that the arrangements for
            the transfer of the deeds are completely legally watertight.

RISPOLO: Lazar Elizarich – I am your servant, my wife, children,
            are your slaves!

LAZAR: A hundred in silver now, and the rest on . . . completion
            of the matter.

RISPOLO: Why didn't God put more people like you on the earth?
            I will pray for you every day. I will kiss the soil where you
            have trod. *(He does so.)*

LAZAR: All right, all right. Listen, this is the way things stand.
            Are you listening? This morning Samson Bolshov and I
            went into town to see his creditors. We took with us this
            document you drew up, offering twenty-five kopecks to
            the rouble. Not one of them would agree to it. Not one!

RISPOLO: Jesus.

LAZAR: Yes. That's the situation. We must look a right pair of
            arseholes. How do you propose I get out of it?

RISPOLO: You can't. I'm afraid you're now obliged to declare
            yourself insolvent.

LAZAR: No, Bolshov's obliged to declare himself insolvent. What
            is *my* position?

RISPOLO: Well . . . *(Laughs)* You've got the deeds to the house . . .
            and the shops . . .

LAZAR: What are you suggesting . . . ?

RISPOLO: It was only a joke.

LAZAR: It wasn't very funny. Don't make that joke again.

RISPOLO: Oh, silly me. My lips are sealed, Lazar.

LAZAR: As a matter of fact I've got something far more attractive
                on my mind than this old house. Come up to my room.
                I want to talk to you about it. Tishka!

                Enter Tishka.

                Clear up. – Let's go. *(Exit)*

                Tishka tries to clear away the vodka.

RISPOLO: Just a minute, young man! Just a bloody minute there!
                You stupid peasant. Do you normally clear away before
                the guests have finished drinking? You may be young,
                but where are your manners? Eh? *(He takes the bottle and
                exits.)*

                *Tishka clears the table. Ustinya and Fominishna enter.
                Tishka exits.*

FOMINISHNA: Do try and get her what she wants, Ustinya. The girl's at
                her wits' end. Half mad with longing if you ask me. She's
                young. She's firm and well-proportioned, like a . . . like a
                turnip. I was married when I was thirteen. I know all
                about . . . *it.*

USTINYA: I can provide suitors in droves. It's you people who are so
                damn choosy.

FOMINISHNA: Rubbish. As long as they're not too old, or too bald, or
                too smelly, they're just men, and they all look much the
                same to me.

USTINYA: *(Sits)* I've been on the go since before dawn. Covered the
                city. A thousand streets! I have to be everywhere – for
                everyone has human needs, haven't they? A girl needs a
                husband; a man needs a wife. One strives to bring them
                together. Well someone has to fix things up. Why?
                Because not everybody in the world knows everybody else

in the world, do they? But – I admit – I do hope to be
remembered for my trouble when the happy day is over.
Someone might give me a length of velvet for a dress,
someone else a pretty shawl, a third might have a bonnet.
Every once in a while I strike lucky. The palm of my hand
loves the soft kiss of gold. Sit down, Fominishna, rest
your poor old legs.

FOMINISHNA: I can't. No time. It's awful here. We all live in fear that
the old man will come home drunk. And then he . . .
When he's late he . . . sometimes . . . He's a terrible
sight! Sleeps with his eyes open! There on the chaise
longue! With alcohol he behaves as peculiar as the very
devil.

USTINYA: I'm told it's easier to understand the devil than a rich
peasant.

FOMINISHNA: I've seen him in a truly dreadful state. Really rather nasty.
One night last week he staggered in completely sloshed.
He said he was going to kill us! Lord alone knows why.
He broke half the crockery instead.

USTINYA: He is uncouth.

FOMINISHNA: He certainly is. I must run upstairs and see Agrafena,
she's all on her own. You rest yourself. Come to me before
you go home, I'll parcel you up some boiled ham.

USTINYA: Jolly decent of you, thank you.

                Exit Fominishna.

                Peasant.

                Enter Lazar.

LAZAR: Ustinya Naumovna, I haven't seen you for ages.

USTINYA: How do you do, young man. You look as fit as ever.

LAZAR: Oh, I'm fit all right.

USTINYA: I'll find you a fit mamzelle if you wish.

LAZAR: Thank you very much, but I've no real need of one at present.

USTINYA: Perhaps one of your friends has? No doubt you have many friends in town . . . ?

LAZAR: As many as a dog, ma'am.

USTINYA: You're lucky. You bring me one of your canine acquaintances – I'll get him a mate before he can bark.

LAZAR: . . . To what purpose do you call at this address so regularly, Ustinya?

USTINYA: Mind your own business. It's quite legal.

LAZAR: I'm just curious. I'm a very curious boy. Are you sure it's worth your while?

USTINYA: Of course it's worth my while! I've found a first-rate suitor! He's of noble stock. He owns serfs. And he's presentable.

LAZAR: How come everything's ground to a halt, then?

USTINYA: Everything has not ground to a halt, what are you twittering about? He's coming round tonight to pay his respects. He'll speak to Mr. Bolshov. I fully expect the proceedings to be concluded on the spot.

LAZAR: The moment he speaks to Bolshov, he'll be off like a rocket.

USTINYA: You're insane!

LAZAR: Wait and see.

USTINYA: . . . Do you know something I don't?

LAZAR: I know what I know.

USTINYA:	And what's that, if one may ask?
LAZAR:	More than you people give me credit for.
USTINYA:	Will your tongue drop off if you tell your friend Ustinya?
LAZAR:	No. But if I do, she'll blurt it out all over the place, won't she?
USTINYA:	No fear! Not me! Cut off my hand if I breathe a word.
LAZAR:	Now that's the kind of bargain I like.
USTINYA:	Speak, then, damn you.
LAZAR:	. . . Is it completely impossible to get rid of this well-bred suitor?
USTINYA:	You are insane. I'm leaving.
LAZAR:	Wait – I've got a friend who's a merchant and he's desperately, urgently in love with Lipochka and he'd give any money to have her.
USTINYA:	Why didn't you say so before?
LAZAR:	I've only just discovered it myself.
USTINYA:	But it's too late now!
LAZAR:	Oh, but Ustinya, this fellow, he'll deluge you with gold, he'll pamper you, he'll make you a coat out of fox fur!
USTINYA:	Fox fur. – Sable?
LAZAR:	All right, sable. Live sables!
USTINYA:	Don't, it's too tempting.
LAZAR:	As you wish.
USTINYA:	I've given my word! My reputation's at stake!

LAZAR: *(Disappointed)* I understand.

USTINYA: Well *actually* I have laid it on a bit thick – that this chap's
                rich, handsome, lovesick and so on . . . When really he's
                . . . But how am I to put Samson Bolshov off? You know
                how stubborn he is. He'll chew me up and spit out the
                gristle.

LAZAR: He'll do no such thing. I'll see to it. Don't you want two
                thousand roubles and a brand-new sable coat? All you've
                got to do is swap suitors. Wedding still goes ahead.
                Matchmaking details we keep strictly between ourselves.
                This man I know is going up and up. The only problem
                is, he's not of noble birth.

USTINYA: So? How many aristocrats have pure blue blood?
                Nowadays every pretty girl in pigtails aspires to be a
                duchess. Take our Lipochka for example. She acts as if
                she was high-born, doesn't she, but not to put too fine a
                point on it, Lazar, her origins are worse than mine and,
                very possibly, yours. Her father used to trade in leather
                mittens – without linings! – on the Balchug. People
                called him Slippery Sam Bolshov and beat the daylight
                out of him whenever they got the opportunity. The old
                girl – Agrafena – is herself barely a cut above peasant
                stock. He plucked her from some mud-hut village, they
                scraped a few roubles together, and before you know it
                they've slithered into the middle class. So the daughter
                thinks she's practically bloody royal! It's only money.
                She's no better than me really. As for her upbringing –
                heaven preserve us. Her handwriting looks like an
                elephant jumped in the inkpot and then crawled round
                the page on its belly. Her French is execrable. And have
                you *seen* her dance?

LAZAR: For all those reasons, I'd say you ought to match her to a
                merchant.

USTINYA: But what shall I do with the suitor I've got? I've told him
                she's a real beauty. Like an oil painting, I implied. And
                all the nonsense about the French and the education and
                . . . oh, dear. What shall I say to him now?

LAZAR: Say exactly the same. But add that she's lost all her
            money. You won't see him for dust.

USTINYA: I can't say that! I've already casually mentioned that
            Samson Bolshov has so much money he can scarcely
            count it.

LAZAR: You're all mouth, Ustinya. How do you know how much
            Bolshov's worth? Have you done an audit?

USTINYA: Anyone will tell you that he is one of the wealthiest men
            in town.

LAZAR: You believe that gossip?

USTINYA: Naturally!

LAZAR: Just shows how much you know. What do you think is
            going to happen if you contract a marriage with this fine
            nobleman and then he discovers Bolshov hasn't got a
            kopeck? He'll say, 'How dare you treat me like a
            tradesman! I will not be swindled out of my rightful
            dowry!' And since he's a man of substance, he's more
            than liable to take you to court. And since a man of
            substance invariably gets what he wants in the courts,
            as you well know, ma'am, you will be sunk up to your
            delightful neck in –

USTINYA: Stop! I don't want to hear any more! I'm confused.

LAZAR: You're scared.

USTINYA: I'm confused!

LAZAR: Take a hundred as deposit, and let's shake on it.

USTINYA: . . . We're still talking two thousand silver roubles and
            a lovely sable coat?

LAZAR: Live sables. Choose your own fur.

USTINYA: Oh, I say, wait till I walk down the High Street in that!

LAZAR: Everyone will think you're a Major-General's wife.

USTINYA: Yes. Their mouths will hang open and they'll dribble.
             They'll envy me so much their noses will drop off.

LAZAR: Dead right they will.

USTINYA: I'll take this on deposit, then . . . ?

LAZAR: Don't lose your nerve.

USTINYA: Don't forget my coat. Oh, you're a charming boy! Let me
             get cracking. I'll give you a full report later.

LAZAR: Hold on! Come up to my room for a vodka. There are one
             or two details about Miss Olimpiada that my friend the
             businessman would like to know. For buying her presents
             and so forth. Tishka! Tishka, get in here!

             Enter Tishka.

TISHKA: Boss?

LAZAR: Keep watch for me. First sign of the old man, I want
             a warning.

TISHKA: Got it.

             *Exit Lazar and Ustinya. Tishka takes money from his
             pocket.*

             Half a rouble that Lazar just give me. Ten kopecks
             donated by Mme. Bolshov the other day when I fell off
             the bell-tower. Then twenty-five kopecks won very
             skilfully at dice. And the day before yesterday the old
             man left a whole silver rouble lying on the counter. Now
             this is what I call money! – I'm on the way to an
             enormous fortune. *(Counts it.)*

             Enter Fominishna.

FOMINISHNA: Tishka! Tishka! Where are you? What's Lazar up to?

TISHKA: How should I know? He never tells me. Why do you want him?

FOMINISHNA: The master's come home. I saw him banging his head against the gatepost! I think he's drunk! Drunk!

TISHKA: Oh, Christ!

FOMINISHNA: Go and fetch Lazar, quick.

Exit Tishka. Enter Agrafena.

AGRAFENA: What's all the commotion, Fominishna? Is my big bear home?

FOMINISHNA: He's drunk! He's drunk! I know! – I'll barricade the door.

Fominishna bars the door.

BOLSHOV: *(Off)* What's all this? Who put this here? Let me through! This is Samson Bolshov!

FOMINISHNA: I don't care if you're the Archangel Gabriel – you're not coming in!

BOLSHOV: *(Off)* You ridiculous old witch! Have you taken leave of your senses?

Bolshov batters his way in.

FOMINISHNA: Oh you're *sober* Mr. Bolshov. *(To Agrafena.)* He's sober! I am such a silly fool, aren't I? I thought you were coming in ever so slightly tipsy, can you believe it? I do beg your pardon. I must be going potty.

BOLSHOV: Seen that legal eagle today?

FOMINISHNA: Eagle? No, we're having goose. With cabbage soup, corned beef, and potatoes.

BOLSHOV: Have you been at the cooking sherry?

FOMINISHNA: No! I promise! I thought it was quite a wholesome menu, myself.

BOLSHOV: Oh, piss off, woman! *(To Agrafena, who is praying.)* And you!

               Exit Fominishna and Agrafena. Enter Lazar and Tishka.

               Lazar –

               Enter Fominishna.

FOMINISHNA: We can have suckling-pig if you prefer – ?

BOLSHOV: Out! Get out! Talk to your pigs!

               Exit Fominishna.

               Has that solicitor been today?

LAZAR: Yes, sir.

BOLSHOV: *(To Tishka.)* Why the fuck are you standing there with your gob open? Got no work to do?

LAZAR: You heard what Mr. Bolshov said! Move!

               Exit Tishka.

BOLSHOV: Did you speak to him?

LAZAR: Sir, don't tell me you credit Rispolozhensky with intelligence. He's no more than a jumped-up secretary. I'm afraid his only advice is 'declare yourself bankrupt'.

BOLSHOV: Well, if it's bankruptcy, then bankruptcy it is. Finish.

LAZAR: Mr. Bolshov, what are you saying?

BOLSHOV: What do you suggest I do? Pay the stinking bastards in full? I'd rather burn everything I've got than give those robbers a kopeck. I'll even go to gaol if I have to!

LAZAR: Good Lord, sir – only a few days ago this was a healthy, thriving establishment. Are you genuinely prepared to let the whole concern run on the rocks?

BOLSHOV: Why should you worry? It's not your affair. Keep up the good work as long as you can. I shan't forget you.

LAZAR: You've treated me well. But sir – you're getting somewhat long in the tooth, if I may say so, with respect. And with the greatest respect, Mme. Bolshov is flagging a bit herself, poor old creature. And you do have certain other responsibilities. Miss Olimpiada –

BOLSHOV: Who?

LAZAR: Lipochka, your daughter – is of an age –

BOLSHOV: What?

LAZAR: Is a very highly cultivated lady, sir, whose interests you are obliged to look after, and who is approaching an age –

BOLSHOV: Oh, don't worry about those two, Lazar. They're my problem.

LAZAR: Yes, I know they are, sir, but – will you listen to *me* for a minute? – the situation looks so dodgy that I must recommend you give Miss Olimpiada away now to a good, reliable man, sir, whilst there's still time! Get four solid walls around her! Get someone resolute and steadfast and true. Not like that fly-by-night nob.

BOLSHOV: What do you mean, fly-by-night?

LAZAR: You'd not heard? He's lost his nerve.

BOLSHOV: Impossible!

LAZAR: I'm sorry. He's absconded. Ask Ustinya.

BOLSHOV: The bastard! What a bloody cheek!

LAZAR: You're better off without him. To turn down an
            indescribable beauty such as your daughter, sir, proves he
            was not a man with taste.

BOLSHOV: Hell, I'm not going to cry over it. *(Pause)* I appreciate
            your concern very much indeed. You're a good lad.

LAZAR: I know I'm an outsider. Not one of the family. But I really
            am worried, Mr. Bolshov, truly. I do fret over the fate of
            Miss Olimpiada, who I hold to be the uniquest young
            woman in the world, and –

BOLSHOV: The uniquest young woman in the world? Did you say
            that?

LAZAR: Did I say that? Oh . . . well . . . just slipped off the
            tongue.

BOLSHOV: You're not in love with my daughter Lipochka, are you?

LAZAR: Please, don't mock me, I'm only a clerk.

BOLSHOV: Well, it's not as if she's the Tsar of Russia's daughter,
            is it?

LAZAR: But you are my benefactor, sir, I have looked up to you in
            place of my own father – no, Mr. Bolshov, it seems
            somehow wrong, I wouldn't be so ungrateful.

BOLSHOV: Oh. You don't love her then.

LAZAR: I never said that! How could I not love her?

BOLSHOV: So you do love her?

LAZAR: It's really not possible for me to –

BOLSHOV: Look, do you or don't you?

LAZAR: More than anything on earth.

BOLSHOV: Good, we're getting somewhere.

LAZAR: I'm sorry . . . I couldn't help it . . . Day after day I watch her from afar . . . night after night I . . . And I'm so insignificant! And also, as you see, so very ugly.

BOLSHOV: You're not particularly ugly. Anyway it's brains that count. You've got your quota of them. Right then: Lazar and Lipochka, up to the altar, is it?

LAZAR: She may not accept me.

BOLSHOV: Sod that. She'll wed who I tell her to, and no tantrums. She's mine, she's my blood. I'll eat her for breakfast if I want. Well, that's enough discussion of the matter, sir. I conclude you desire my daughter's hand in marriage. You can have it. And, for her dowry, I'll turn over everything I've got to you.

LAZAR: Oh, sir, there's no need for –

BOLSHOV: Yes. Those bloody creditors will be sorry they didn't take twenty-five kopecks when they had the chance.

LAZAR: They'll be sorry all right.

BOLSHOV: That's the ticket! Off you go and take care of the shops, now, Lazar. But this evening, come back here. I'll introduce you to your bride and your mother-in-law. Wait till we see their faces . . . !

LAZAR: *(Laughing)* I'm looking forward to it. Father.

END OF ACT TWO

ACT THREE

Bolshov's house. Food and drink.

BOLSHOV: *(In his favourite armchair. Looks round the room. Yawns.)* This is it, then, is it? Life? *(Pause)* 'Vanity of vanities; all is vanity.' Ecclesiastes One, verse Two. And never was a truer word spoke. Damnation, I can't make up my mind what to do. I rather fancy a bite to eat – but I'd spoil my dinner. If I stay sat here I'll fall asleep. Then I'll be awake all night. Perhaps I'll have a nice cup of tea. *(Pause)* Perhaps not. *(Pause)* Well, there you are, then. You live for a little while and then you die. Ashes to ashes, dust to dust – a daft saying if ever I heard one. O God, O God, I'm so bored. *(Yawns)*

> *Enter Agrafena, Lipochka, Fominishna, Tishka. Lipochka is in her corsets. The others prepare to try and lace her up and get her into an extraordinary, voluminous dress. Bolshov looks horrified.*

AGRAFENA: Come along in, my pretty. Samson, come and admire the gorgeous frock we're going to put on your daughter!

> *They begin to dress Lipochka. She is shoved and squeezed.*

Oh, she's such an angel. Such a princess! All she needs now, Samson, is a coach and six white horses to carry her around.

BOLSHOV: She can have two brown ones like anybody else.

AGRAFENA: Well, she may not be a General's daughter, but that's not *her* fault. She is possessed of dazzling beauty, all the same.

FOMINISHNA: Ready? Heave! *(She and Tishka tug at the corset. Lipochka gasps for breath.)*

AGRAFENA: Why can't you be pleasant to the child, you old grizzly bear?

BOLSHOV: Pleasant? What do you want me to do, kiss the soles of
             her feet? Why are you making such a fuss and
             performance? I've seen plenty of girls dressed up to the
             nines before now.

AGRAFENA: Oh, have you? And where have you seen them? When
             you're away on business? – I'm not talking about those
             kind of girls, I'm talking about your own flesh and blood.

BOLSHOV: *(Sourly)* Oh.

LIPOCHKA: Pull, Tishka!

             *They can't get her corset laced up. Lipochka turns to
             Bolshov.*

             Punch me, daddy.

             *Bolshov punches her in the stomach. It knocks the wind
             out of her and she succeeds in lacing up her corset. All
             gasp in admiration.*

AGRAFENA: *(To Bolshov.)* You've got a heart of stone, you.

BOLSHOV: So she's my daughter. So what? Just give thanks she's got
             boots on her feet, clothes on her back, and meat in her
             belly. I can't think what more she could want.

AGRAFENA: What more she could want . . . ? Are you totally
             insensitive? It's our *duty* to feed her. It says so in the
             Gospels. And we'd do the same for any stranger in need.
             But this is your own daughter we're talking about!

LIPOCHKA: *(Being dressed.)* Look, mummy!

BOLSHOV: I know it is! What are you suggesting, we put her in a
             picture-frame and hang her on the wall? God, you go on
             and on. It's transparently obvious I am her father, isn't
             that enough?

AGRAFENA: No. It's about time you faced up to reality. Soon we shall
             be losing her. And you've nothing to say. Can't you give

her a few useful *facts* . . . ? About *life*? Oh, Lord give me
patience, you have no paternal instincts at all, have you?

BOLSHOV: No, I haven't. It's the way I was made.

They have succeeded in getting Lipochka into the dress.

AGRAFENA: There! She's in! Oh, she looks just like a – a geranium,
doesn't she? *(Lipochka sighs.)* But you treat her as if she
was an animal. Speak to her. Go on. Have a conversation
with her.

BOLSHOV: Have a conversation with her? Have you gone mad?

AGRAFENA: Very well, if that's your attitude, I've got something to
tell you. We have a very important visitor coming, so
make sure you behave. It will be his first soirée at our gaff
and as a matter of fact we don't yet know what he looks
like.

BOLSHOV: *(Gets out his newspaper.)* Oh, belt up, woman.

AGRAFENA: Call yourself a father? I don't know how you managed it,
you're so ill-equipped. Poor, poor little Lipochka, stood
there like an orphan with her head hung down. And
you – big brute! He'd sling you out with the pigswill,
wouldn't he, my precious? Sit down, now. Sit down.

Agrafena forces Lipochka to sit.

LIPOCHKA: Oh, leave off, ma! Look, you've ruined my
comportment!

AGRAFENA: I'll mend it for you, sweetheart.

LIPOCHKA: *(Shrieks)* No!

AGRAFENA: Then I'll stand over here and just look.

LIPOCHKA: Why must you meddle? You're a squawky old chicken.

AGRAFENA: *(Tearful)* I'm just going to be so sorry to lose you . . . !

LIPOCHKA: You knew it would happen one day. You've had plenty of
             time to get adjusted.

AGRAFENA: I'm still going to feel sad. You've been living with us for
             years and years and years and now all of a sudden you're
             gone.

             Grunt of pleasure from Bolshov.

             And to a perfect stranger! There seems no logic in it.
             It's as if for some odd reason we'd had enough of your
             petulance, your silly childish tantrums, your racket – and
             so we'll drive you from our doorstep like we'd whip a
             nasty mad person out of town. But one day we'll wake up
             and we'll realise we're at the end of our lives and we've
             nowhere left to go but down. *(To audience.)* Think, ladies
             and gentlemen, think what a desperate existence it will be
             for the girl, living in a far-off part of the land, choking on
             a strange man's bread and every evening wiping away the
             tears with her little fist . . . it's unbearable! For the love
             of God, she's going to the wrong fellow, surely! *(Weeps)*
             She's marrying some idiot, some inbred idiot, doesn't
             deserve her, forced his way into our tight-knit family
             group, a brutal idiot and the son of a rat!

BOLSHOV: What the creeping Jesus are you going on about? What
             idiot? What rat?

AGRAFENA: I had to say it – it all came flooding out. *(To audience.)*
             Sorry.

BOLSHOV: Tears come cheap with you, don't they?

LIPOCHKA: *(To Agrafena.)* You should be ashamed. He'll be here in
             a minute. Try and keep yourself under control.

AGRAFENA: Yes, dear.

             A knock on the door. Consternation. Ustinya enters.

USTINYA: Good day to you all. May I come in?

BOLSHOV: You are in.

USTINYA: Why does everyone look so awfully gloomy?

AGRAFENA: We've been waiting a very long time. Thank you, Tishka.

              Exit Tishka.

LIPOCHKA: Is he here, Ustinya?

USTINYA: I have a confession to make. It's my fault, I accept the
              blame. But there's a hitch.

LIPOCHKA: What? What do you mean?

USTINYA: It's the suitor I'm afraid. He's gone cold on us.

LIPOCHKA: Oh, no! *(She swoons.)*

BOLSHOV: *(Laughs)* Call yourself a matchmaker? You couldn't
              match a pair of dogs in heat!

USTINYA: I'm sorry. He's gone all sensitive and, well, indecisive.

AGRAFENA: Oh, Lord! When did you last talk to him?

USTINYA: This morning. I had myself announced at his house. He
              came out to the drawing-room still in his dressing-gown!
              He did give me a bite to eat, though, and quite delicious
              it was too, and appropriately high-class – you know,
              Agrafena, coffee with rum, and chocolate, and lots and
              lots of fancy Italian biscuits. 'Tuck in,' he said, 'as much
              as you want.' I pigged myself. But I'd gone to talk
              business, after all. So I said, 'We've got to come to a
              decision, haven't we?' He went rather quiet. 'I'll think
              about it,' was the best I could get. Just sat there fiddling
              with the cords on his dressing-gown.

              Lipochka comes to.

LIPOCHKA: Do you mean he was referring to me and he hadn't even
              bothered to get dressed . . . ! What's he playing at?

AGRAFENA: It's affected. That's what it is.

USTINYA: Good riddance to bad rubbish, I say. Look here, why
                don't we get you another?

BOLSHOV: Because it'll be the same damn thing all over again, that's
                why. No, this time *I'll* find her a man.

LIPOCHKA: Oh, no!

AGRAFENA: Where are you going to find a suitor, when you spend all
                your life flopped on your arse in front of the stove?

BOLSHOV: You leave it to me.

AGRAFENA: Oh, Samson, don't start talking in that tone of voice, you
                know the chances are I'll get upset . . .

                *Bolshov laughs. Agrafena sits, disconsolate. Ustinya
                takes Lipochka aside.*

USTINYA: Well, aren't we dressed up? My word, that thing does
                flatter you, doesn't it. Did you make it yourself?

LIPOCHKA: What a revolting idea! What do you think we are,
                paupers? What do you suppose we have dressmakers for?

USTINYA: I never suggested you were paupers! I'd never say a thing
                like that. Look at the house, the furnishings – it's quite
                obvious you wouldn't need to run up your own frocks.
                Good God no. But none the less – it still looks, I don't
                quite know how to put it, common on you.

LIPOCHKA: How dare you! Common? You're so ignorant! Common?
                Have you been afflicted by a sudden attack of blindness?

USTINYA: Calm down, my dear.

LIPOCHKA: I shouldn't have to put up with you. You think I'm
                uncouth, don't you? Well you're wrong. Pig!

USTINYA: You take offence too easily, Lipochka! You didn't think I
                was criticising your dress, did you? It is only a dress after
                all. What I meant was that it doesn't suit you as well as it

might. It doesn't bring out your true inner beauty. I think actually that a delicate broderie anglaise – here – might be better, with, let's see, enormous pearls? Here? Ah, you're smiling. Pearls, absolutely! Your friend Ustinya knows what she's talking about.

Enter Tishka.

TISHKA: The solicitor Rispolozhensky has asked me to ask if he may ask to come in. He's outside with Lazar Elizarich.

BOLSHOV: Tell him to come on in – and bring Lazar.

Exit Tishka.

AGRAFENA: I don't want these tasty snacks to go to waste. Everybody come and eat some. Ustinya, will you take a tiny weeny vodka?

USTINYA: Yes, please. The best people always take a glass at this hour, you know.

AGRAFENA: Do they? Samson Bolshov, move your behind, so we can get at the scoff.

BOLSHOV: Hold on. The others aren't here yet.

LIPOCHKA: I'm going to change my dress, mama.

AGRAFENA: Off you go, child.

BOLSHOV: Wait. You're not changing anything. A new suitor's on his way.

AGRAFENA: A new suitor? Oh, go on, you – stop messing around.

LIPOCHKA: I think perhaps I'll hang on just in case, mama. *(Checks her hair.)* Father . . . there's something I ought to mention to you.

BOLSHOV: Oh? What?

LIPOCHKA: Dear father – I'm ashamed to say it.

AGRAFENA: Don't be ashamed – spit it out.

USTINYA: Being ashamed never hurt anybody.

AGRAFENA: I expect she wants a new hat, Samson.

LIPOCHKA: It's not a hat. I don't want a hat.

BOLSHOV: What do you want, then?

LIPOCHKA: A soldier, I want to marry a soldier.

AGRAFENA: Oh you silly trollop – you're for the high jump now.

LIPOCHKA: But why? Other girls marry army men.

BOLSHOV: Other girls can do what they want.

Enter Lazar and Rispolozhensky.

RISPOLO: How do you do, Mr. Bolshov. Mme. Bolshov, you look
                charming. Miss Lipochka. You look charming too.

BOLSHOV: Good evening, brother Rispolozhensky. Come along in
                and sit down. You too, Lazar.

AGRAFENA: You will have something to eat? I've had a horses'
                d'oeuvres made up.

RISPOLO: Yes, of course. And given the warmth of the occasion a
                small vodka wouldn't go amiss.

BOLSHOV: In a moment we'll go in to dine. But first, I'd like some
                herring and pickles and a good straightforward chat.

USTINYA: Super idea!

Total silence for quite some time.

Do you know I read in one of the cheaper newspapers

today – didn't buy it, found it in the gutter – that there's been another revolution in Europe.

BOLSHOV: Revolution is not on the agenda.

USTINYA: What, if one may ask, is permitted subject matter?

BOLSHOV: Old age. And what comes after that. And the fact that our health gets worse and worse every bloody minute of every bloody day. God alone knows what's in store for us. And so we have resolved, whilst we're still compos mentis, to hand over our only daughter to holy matrimony. As for her dowry, we trust that she won't besmirch our reputation, but will behave herself and button her lip, specially in front of guests.

USTINYA: What an accomplished speaker you are. All the words in the right order and everything.

BOLSHOV: And now, since our only daughter is conveniently to hand, and being apprised of the honourable intentions and complete financial self-sufficiency of our future son-in-law, which for us is a matter of some gratification, and seeing as how we want to be publicly seen to be blessing this union of souls, we shall name the lucky fellow forthwith. Lipochka, come here.

LIPOCHKA: Why, father?

BOLSHOV: Come on, I'm not going to bite your head off. You as well, Lazar. Stand up on your two hind legs, eh?

LAZAR: I'm up, sir. I've been waiting for this for a long, long time.

BOLSHOV: *(To Lipochka.)* Give me your hand.

LIPOCHKA: What is this? Party games?

BOLSHOV: It'll be worse for you if I have to use force.

USTINYA: Oh no.

FOMINISHNA: You're done for now, my girl.

LIPOCHKA: . . . I won't! I can't! Marry such a – thing! Ugh,
                repulsive!

LAZAR: Just as I feared, sir – she won't have me. It's not to be.

BOLSHOV: *(Forcibly takes Lipochka's hand. And takes Lazar's.)* Not to
                be? Not to be? If I want it to be, it will be! Daughter – I
                feed you, you obey me.

AGRAFENA: What a terrible thing to say! Please, Samson, come to
                your senses.

BOLSHOV: Keep out of this, this is not women's business. Lipochka,
                here is your bridegroom. Love and honour him and all of
                that. Now, you two sit down on the couch and whisper
                sweet nothings to one another. We'll go next door and
                plan the wedding.

LIPOCHKA: I'm not sitting next to that creep! Jesus!

BOLSHOV: You can either sit down of your own free will, or I can
                thrash the arse off you!

LIPOCHKA: A refined person can't marry an employee of the firm, it's
                unheard of!

BOLSHOV: Silence! Or I'll wed you to Fedot down the road!

                Silence.

USTINYA: I've never heard of anything like it, Agrafena. Smells like
                trouble to me.

AGRAFENA: I haven't a clue what's going on, it's all a blur. How in the
                world did we come to such a muddle?

FOMINISHNA: Yes, I've seen some weddings in my time, but never a
                muck-up like this.

AGRAFENA: You wicked, wicked men, what do you think you're
             doing? Humiliating this young girl! *(She beats Bolshov.)*

BOLSHOV: You do talk some horseshit, wife! I have decided to marry
             my daughter to my clerk, and if that's what I've decided,
             so shall it be. I'm not in a mood to debate. So why don't
             we all go in and eat whilst they get to know each other?

RISPOLO: I'm with you, Mr. Bolshov, and if you need a proposer for
             a good luck toast, sir, you know where to turn. The first
             duty of any child, my dear Agrafena, is to obey its
             parents. That rule didn't start with us, and it won't stop
             with us, either.

                    They all exit except Lazar, Lipochka and Agrafena.

LIPOCHKA: *(Weeping)* Mama, mama, what does it mean? Does he
             want me to spend the rest of my days in the kitchen with
             the staff?

AGRAFENA: There, there.

LAZAR: Mme. Bolshov . . . Mother . . . You'll never find another
             son-in-law like me. I'll show respect. I'll look after you in
             your old age. Remember, ma'am, the young lady's
             previous suitor did not want to know you. To him you
             were stinking trash. Whereas I, ma'am, will be forever
             grateful for this match. And I will honour and support
             you until the day I die.

AGRAFENA: Lord Almighty, I've gone all weak.

BOLSHOV: *(Off)* Wife, come here!

                    Agrafena goes to leave. Lipochka tries to cling on to her.

LAZAR: Please remember what I have just said to you, ma'am.

                    Exit Agrafena. Pause.

LAZAR: Olimpiada –

LIPOCHKA: *(Sulkily)* What?

LAZAR: Olimpiada, gracious Olimpiada – do you genuinely
                despise me? Speak to me. Say one word.

LIPOCHKA: Moron.

LAZAR: Why do you insult me, Olimpiada?

LIPOCHKA: I'll tell you once and for all. I'll never marry you.

LAZAR: I cannot force your love. But I would like to say that I –

LIPOCHKA: I'm not listening. Push off! You're some lover, you are.
                Hah! I wouldn't marry you if you were a millionaire!
                You'll have to withdraw.

LAZAR: And then, if I withdraw – ?

LIPOCHKA: I'll marry a nobleman.

LAZAR: They tend not to take brides who have no dowries. As a
                rule.

LIPOCHKA: What do you mean, no dowries? What awful rubbish you
                talk. If you caught a glimpse of my dowry, why it'd knock
                you over backwards!

LAZAR: Oh, you mean your clothes? Yes, they certainly are
                disarming. But a nobleman will not buy solely on the
                basis of the packaging, Olimpiada. Your little strips of
                ribbon and lace will never substitute for money.

LIPOCHKA: So what? If they want money, daddy will give it to them.

LAZAR: That would be quite in order if he had any to give. But
                you don't know the firm's affairs as I do, miss. I have to
                tell you that your father is bankrupt.

LIPOCHKA: Bankrupt?

LAZAR: Broke.

LIPOCHKA:	What about the house and the shops?
LAZAR:	The house and the shops are mine.
LIPOCHKA:	Yours?
LAZAR:	Yes.
LIPOCHKA:	Are you mocking me? Is this your idea of a practical joke? Because if so, you can find yourself a girl who's more gullible!
LAZAR:	I have the papers.
LIPOCHKA:	You have bought them from father . . . ?
LAZAR:	He mortgaged them to me, yes . . .
LIPOCHKA:	Oh, these stupid peasants! What have they done? They brought me up nicely, gave me a decent education, introduced me to all the finer things in life, and now the idiots have gone and bankrupted themselves!
LAZAR:	Olimpiada . . . let's assume for a minute that you do marry an aristocrat. Where would it get you? You would have the advantage of being free to call yourself a Lady. But none of the fun that goes with it. Think. Use your brain. Haven't you ever seen the females of the impoverished nobility going to market to buy their own groceries? On foot? And if they do one day indulge in the extravagance of driving somewhere, their four horses are all an elaborate show, for if you look closely, as I have, you'll see that these horses are in worse condition than a merchant's nag. And compared to yourself, miss, what kind of a way do these ladies dress? Not exactly comparable is it? But if you marry me, dear Olimpiada, I swear to you on my mother's grave, you'll wear pure silk gowns around the house, you'll never go in less than velvet to pay your calls or sit in our box at the theatre, and as far as hats and coats are concerned, why, within six months the gentry will be following *you*. Your clothes will come from Paris! Your horses from the Orlov stud! *(Pause)*

If it is my appearance which you have reservations about, ma'am, then I assure you your requirements can be accommodated. I would not say no to attiring myself in a nice frock coat. I will even shave my beard. If that is what you want.

LIPOCHKA: You men are all the same. Promise the whole world before the wedding. But after you've had your way, you cheat us.

LAZAR: Kill me on the spot if I was to think so base a thought! Damn me to hell and back, if I'm lying! I have respect for you. I wouldn't cheat you, ever. We don't have to go on living in this old house, you know. We'll set ourselves up in one of the new streets, and we'll have the ceilings painted with birds of paradise, and lilac trees, and the little fat fellow with the bow and arrow, what's his name?

LIPOCHKA: Cupid.

LAZAR: Yes, Cupid!

LIPOCHKA: Cupids aren't in vogue any more.

LAZAR: Christ, you can have Eros then! Look I'm no good at paying pretty compliments. But I do – desire you.

LIPOCHKA: . . . Do you speak French, Lazar Elizarich?

LAZAR: No.

LIPOCHKA: Why not?

LAZAR: I've never had the remotest use for it. Olimpiada, please, make me a happy man. I've never been happy in my life. Tell me you accept my proposal. *(Pause)* Order me to kneel before you.

LIPOCHKA: Kneel!

Lazar kneels.

Oh, what a ghastly waistcoat.

LAZAR:	I'll give it to Tishka. I'll get a new one made at the tailor's of your choice. Don't reject me, I'll die! *(Pause)* Well, Olimpiada?
LIPOCHKA:	Let me think it over.
LAZAR:	Why do you need to think it over?
LIPOCHKA:	Why shouldn't I think it over?
LAZAR:	But you don't need to think!
LIPOCHKA:	Oh, don't you allow it?
LAZAR:	It's just not necessary!
LIPOCHKA:	Lazar, I've got an idea.
LAZAR:	Anything!
LIPOCHKA:	Let's elope.
LAZAR:	. . . Elope? What, run away? But . . . your father's given his permission.
LIPOCHKA:	Everybody elopes for their marriage these days, it's the fashion.
LAZAR:	Well I'm sorry, but I have to draw the line at something.
LIPOCHKA:	Oh. I see. Well, if you're so dull that you won't sweep me off my feet and marry me in secret, I suppose we'll just have to go ahead with the normal tedious method.
LAZAR:	Olimpiada . . . ?

He looks questioningly to her. Slowly it dawns on them both that she's just agreed to marry him.

Olimpiada! Christ! Let me kiss your hand!

*He kisses her hand, her arm. Then they give each other
a first quick tremulous kiss on the lips. They pull apart,
stunned.*

LIPOCHKA: Lazar! Lazar, come here!

LAZAR: What is it?

LIPOCHKA: *(She grips him.)* If you only knew what a life I have in this
              house . . . ! My mother tells me to do one thing one
              minute, another the next. When my father's not drunk
              he never says a word, and when he is drunk he'll beat you
              up as soon as look at you. How is a lady of refinement
              supposed to live with it? If I could have married into the
              nobility, I could have left home and forgotten all about it.
              But now things will go on just exactly as before.

LAZAR: No they won't, Olimpiada. As soon as we're properly
              married we'll move into a new house, like I said. And
              then no-one can tell us how we ought to live. Put all this
              behind you! We'll give the orders from now on.

LIPOCHKA: You're too timid. You'll never stand up to father. A
              nobleman would have come to some understanding.

LAZAR: I may seem to be timid. I am your father's clerk. But
              when we're in our own home you will see what kind of
              a man I am. No powdered fop could love you as I will,
              Lipochka. I will give myself up to your pleasure.

LIPOCHKA: Ooh . . . So look, have I got the terms right? We're
              leaving here, we'll have our own lives, they can have
              theirs, everything we have will be fashionable, they can
              plod on as they like – ?

LAZAR: That's it.

LIPOCHKA: Done. Call father.

LAZAR: Mr. Bolshov, sir! Father!

              Bolshov enters.

LAZAR:	Miss Olimpiada has consented, sir!

Enter Agrafena. They all embrace each other.

AGRAFENA:	I'm coming as fast as I can!
BOLSHOV:	There, what did I tell you? I know what I'm doing. Not a lot you can teach me, Lazar.
LAZAR:	*(To Agrafena.)* Mother . . . ? May I kiss you hand?
AGRAFENA:	Yes, kiss either of them, they're both clean. Oh, my precious! Is everything settled already? That was jolly quick. Well I never! I don't know what to think.
LIPOCHKA:	Mama, I simply never dreamt that Lazar Elizarich was such a courteous and attentive gentleman. He's a lot more considerate than the others.
AGRAFENA:	Well of course he is, you silly! You didn't think your father would do anything that wasn't in your best interests? Oh, it's so romantic, it's like a fairy-tale. *(Screeches)* Fominishna! Fominishna!

Enter Fominishna.

FOMINISHNA:	Coming!
BOLSHOV:	Quiet a minute, you noisy baggage. You two sit down next to each other so we can get a good look at you. Fetch us a bottle of champagne.
FOMINISHNA:	Champagne! Right away, your highness, right away.

Exit Fominishna. Lazar and Lipochka sit. Enter Ustinya and Rispolozhensky.

AGRAFENA:	Ustinya, quick, come and congratulate the happy couple. We're going to have a wedding! Thanks be to God!
USTINYA:	How am I to congratulate them properly without a glass of something in my hand?

RISPOLO: Interesting question.

                Enter Fominishna and Tishka. Tishka has champagne
                on a tray.

BOLSHOV: Here we are, this'll soften your hard bloody hearts.

USTINYA: Well that's more like it! Champagne! May God grant you
                both a very long life, and may you get very rich and very
                fat.

ALL: Very rich, and very fat! *(They drink.)*

USTINYA: What about a kiss from the young lovers, then?

                Lazar and Lipochka kiss rather forcefully.

BOLSHOV: I also wish to propose a toast. May you do very, very, er,
                nicely. You've got the brains for it. And so that you get a
                good start, Lazar, I am making over sole ownership of the
                house and shops to you instead of a dowry.

                Bolshov is congratulated. Rispolozhensky produces the
                legal documents and they are handed over to Lazar.

LAZAR: Gosh, father, that's too much.

BOLSHOV: Not at all. Not for you. They're my goods. I got them
                myself with my own two hands. I'll give them to whoever
                I want. More champagne, Tishka! Let's hear no more
                about it. The odd good deed is not against the law, I
                think. *(Laughs)* Take the lot. Just feed me and my old girl
                here. And pay off the creditors at ten kopecks a rouble.

LAZAR: Only ten?

BOLSHOV: Yes. Teach the sods a lesson. I've often thought how
                peaceful it must be in prison. Quiet, and sort of serene. I
                can catch up on my reading. Whilst those bloody bastards
                sweat. But make sure you pay, when they come down to
                ten, won't you?

LAZAR: It will be my very first duty as your son-in-law. This is a family affair now.

BOLSHOV: Well said, bloody well said, my boy! Right, Tishka, let's have a tune!

Tishka plays on an accordion and everyone joins in the wedding dance.

AGRAFENA: Oh, the sweethearts! I wouldn't have believed it possible. I'm half out of my mind with joy! Sing something for us, Ustinya.

Ustinya sings a sentimental song.

Bolshov offers a glass of champagne to Rispolozhensky, who refuses.

BOLSHOV: Drink to their health and happiness, Rispolozhensky.

RISPOLO: I can't, Mr. Bolshov, champagne makes me ill.

BOLSHOV: Drink! To my children!

USTINYA: He's hopeless isn't he.

RISPOLO: It makes me ill, honestly, and I get drunk on it, you see! If you've a small glass of ordinary vodka I'll gladly join the toast. But I can't take any sort of wine. I have a weak constitution.

USTINYA: Can't take wine, indeed! What a prune! Well if you haven't the good grace to drink it, I think I'll pour it down your neck!

RISPOLO: That's not a nice thing to do, Ustinya! Not a nice thing at all in any respect! Keep off! I just can't swallow it. Do you think I enjoy saying no to a drink? I appreciate how good people behave, and I never refuse a drop of vodka, out of politeness, and if you offered one now I would sink it, will you get away from me? It makes me go peculiar, Mr. Bolshov, and I can't walk straight! I mean not the slightest offence!

BOLSHOV: Let him have it, Ustinya!

                Rispolozhensky runs from her.

RISPOLO: Help! Help!

                Laughter.

                        END OF ACT THREE

ACT FOUR

Lazar's new house. Six months later.

> *A richly furnished room. Enter Lazar and Tishka.*
> *Tishka helps Lazar into a smart new frock coat.*

LAZAR: How's the cut?

TISHKA: Fits you perfect.

LAZAR: What do you reckon then, Tishka? Do I look French?

TISHKA: French to the very letter, sir.

> *Lipochka enters, dressed gorgeously in the latest fashions,*
> *eating chocolates.*

LAZAR: *(He parades round the room.)* Do you not think me rather
stylish, Olimpiada? And you wanted a Guards officer
. . . ! Why all I have to do is buy the latest coat and put it
on correctly, and voy-la! – it's as if I'd worn it all my life.

LIPOCHKA: Still can't dance, though, can you.

LAZAR: I'll learn. You wait. I'll learn every style in the book.
Come the autumn, we'll go to all the Merchants' Guilds'
Assemblies. And me and you will dance the polka. We'll
be astounding!

LIPOCHKA: If you want to go to *those* do's, Lazar, you better buy that
new barouche we saw at Arbatsky's. The one with the
folding roof.

LAZAR: Tishka, see to it.

TISHKA: Very good, sir. *(Exit)*

LAZAR: There, Olimpiada, the barouche is yours.

LIPOCHKA: Do try and take delivery by Friday, so we may drive out to
the country. I've a new cape I want to wear.

LAZAR: By all means, my darling. Whatever your pretty heart
            desires. And then on Sunday we'll drive to the park so
            that everyone can see us. You do realise that barouche will
            cost a thousand roubles, and the horses with the inlaid
            silver harness, approx. a thousand more? Little point in
            leaving the damn thing at home, is there?

            Lazar sits next to Lipochka. They face the audience.

            Yes. That's the spirit, Olimpiada. Let them all have a
            bloody good look.

            Long pause.

LIPOCHKA: Lazar, you haven't kissed me for, oh, ages.

LAZAR: Little darling . . .

            They kiss passionately.

            Speak to me in French, you know I adore it.

LIPOCHKA: What shall I say?

LAZAR: First thing to come into your beautiful head . . .

LIPOCHKA: 'Comme tu es joli, mon amour.'

LAZAR: Delicious. What's it mean?

LIPOCHKA: 'How sweet you are, my love.'

LAZAR: What a fabulous wife I've got. Olimpiada, I'm so proud
            of you, I want to shout for joy! Kiss me again.

            *They kiss hard and clutch at each other. Tishka enters and
            they pull apart.*

TISHKA: Ustinya Naumovna is here.

LAZAR: What the hell does she want? Send her in.

*Tishka exits. Lazar and Lipochka straighten their
clothing. Tishka re-enters with Ustinya.*

TISHKA: *(Formally)* Ustinya Naumovna.

               Exit Tishka.

USTINYA: My dears! You do look well.

LAZAR: No doubt we have been mentioned in your prayers,
               Ustinya.

USTINYA: *(Kisses Lipochka.)* Lipochka, what's all this? Do I detect
               a slight filling out around the middle?

LIPOCHKA: No you do not. Wherever do you get these bizarre ideas
               from, Ustinya Naumovna?

USTINYA: Bizarre? It's the way of the flesh. No point blushing,
               dear. You pay for your pleasure, and no-one escapes.
               Look here, why am I so utterly ignored nowadays? I feel
               quite neglected. Perhaps you haven't a minute to spare for
               your old friends. Too engrossed in each other, I suppose.
               Too busy kissing and cuddling. *(To Lipochka.)* Only the
               best clothes for you now, one can't help but notice. You
               must have money to burn.

LIPOCHKA: I haven't spent that much. It's only because the new
               spring collections have just come out.

USTINYA: What are ladies of fashion going in for this season – wool
               or silk?

LIPOCHKA: It's best to have some of each, really. Not long ago I had
               a dress made of crêpe with gold leaf trimmings.

USTINYA: Good gracious! How many dresses have you altogether,
               do you think?

LIPOCHKA: Well, I shall have to count: there's my wedding dress –
               the off-white with the scarlet overlay – and three velvets,
               that makes four; two gauze and the crêpe with gold leaf

trimmings, seven; three satin and three grosgrain, that's thirteen; another seven in gros de Naples and gros d'Afrique, three marceline, two mousseline, and two chine royal – think two's enough? – I make that twenty-seven. I've got about four more in crêpe Rachel. Then of course I've got my muslins, my bouffe mousselines, and those silly cotton things, twenty or thirty or so, I've lost count. The other day I had a dress made out of some very weird stuff from Persia.

USTINYA: You've quite a collection, haven't you? Why don't you go and see if there's an old gros d'Afrique you won't want any more?

LIPOCHKA: I can't possibly give you a gros d'Afrique dress. I've only got three. I'll give you a crêpe Rachel.

USTINYA: I'm not walking the streets looking like a shopgirl. It's clear that I'm making no progress at all. Give me a satin one and let's have done with it.

LIPOCHKA: The trouble is – my satin ones are all really ball-gowns, they require a degree of, well, *décolletage*, Ustinya, – that means 'bosom' in French – to carry them off. Quite unsuitable for you. I'll gladly find you a housecoat in crêpe Rachel. If we sew extra pleats it should fit you.

USTINYA: . . . I'm sure that will be absolutely delightful. Off you go and rummage in your closets, then.

LIPOCHKA: Yes. It might take me a minute.

USTINYA: I don't mind waiting. I need to talk to your husband, as it happens.

Exit Lipochka.

Well, well, well. Who seems to have forgotten his promise to his friend Ustinya? Naughty boy.

LAZAR: Me forget? I don't forget.

He takes out his wallet and gives her a banknote.

USTINYA: What's this?

LAZAR: A hundred roubles, ma'am.

USTINYA: A hundred roubles? Fifteen hundred, I want.

LAZAR: Sorry?

USTINYA: Fifteen hundred roubles, you promised.

LAZAR: Look, I know you're a grasping old bitch, Ustinya, but
            that's a bit steep even for you.

USTINYA: You wretch. You don't play funny games with me, you
            know. You made me a promise!

LAZAR: Oh, I promise all kinds of things. I promised I'd climb
            up the bell-tower of Ivan the Great if I got into a certain
            someone's drawers. Did I do it? Did I hell. I'm
            changeable. That's what I'm like.

USTINYA: What makes you think I won't sue you for this
            outstanding debt? I might decide to overlook the fact that
            you're a merchant of the second Guild, now, and I'm
            stuck down in the fourteenth rank. I am widow to a
            government official, I'll have you know.

LAZAR: If you were widow to a four-star General, Ustinya
            Naumovna, I would still not give a fuck. I don't want
            to know you any more. I've nothing further to say.

USTINYA: And you also promised me a sable coat.

LAZAR: I didn't.

USTINYA: Yes! Arctic circle sables!

LAZAR: No, I never said that.

USTINYA: Are you losing your memory?

LAZAR: No, it was my friend the merchant said that. I never said any such thing. Are you losing your marbles, Ustinya?

USTINYA: You monster! I'll throttle you!

She goes for him. But Lipochka enters with the dress.

LAZAR: Ustinya hasn't the complexion to bring off a sable coat, has she, darling?

LIPOCHKA: Good Lord no. You shouldn't wear brown, Ustinya, with skin like yours.

USTINYA: Are you trying to rob me?

LIPOCHKA: No, I'm giving you a dress. Here.

LAZAR: If you're going to make accusations of robbery, I think you should leave. We've said all there is to say.

USTINYA: I must have been soft in the head to get mixed up with you. I can see what you are. The blood of the street-urchin dribbles through your veins, doesn't it, Lazar? You cheat. You filthy parasite. You're a common tradesman and you always will be.

LAZAR: *(Yells)* Get out of my house!

USTINYA: With pleasure! And I never want to see you again! Ugh! No money in the world will drag me here from now on. I'm too proud! I'd skirt the whole city before I'd walk down your street. Come round here and watch you two billing and cooing? I'd sooner watch the flies on a dead dog's balls!

LIPOCHKA: If you carry on in that tone of voice in this neighbourhood, Ustinya, we'll have to send for the police.

USTINYA: Oh, I'll carry on, I'll shame you, I'll shout your evil from the rooftops, ooh how I'll yell, you'll never show your bloody selves in public again! To do business with you, I have presumably gone quite insane – me, a lady of legitimate rank! *(She spits at both of them.)*

Exit Ustinya.

LAZAR: Well would you credit it: blue blood boils more easy
than the usual sort. It must've been fun being married to
that. Down there in the fourteenth rank. Look at the old
hag scuttle up the street . . . !

LIPOCHKA: You were the one doing business with her.

LAZAR: An error of judgement. The woman's professionally
incompetent.

LIPOCHKA: *(Looking out of the window.)* Lazar! Look! They've let my
father out of prison!

LAZAR: No, that's not very likely, my sweet. He has to remain
inside until the whole affair is resolved, you see. He has to
be investigated.

LIPOCHKA: But he's coming down the road as large as life!

LAZAR: Christ. Where? – I'll tell you what must have happened.
They've sent him to attend a meeting of his creditors, and
he's got permission to pay us a visit. You better call your
mother.

LIPOCHKA: Mama! Father's coming! Fominishna! Father's coming!

Enter Tishka.

TISHKA: Samson Bolshov's coming, boss.

LAZAR: I know!

Enter Agrafena.

AGRAFENA: Where is he? Oh, my darling, my pet. Where is he?

LAZAR: What a bloody nuisance.

Enter Fominishna.

FOMINISHNA: Wait for me! Wait for me!

               *Tishka announces Bolshov, who enters cheerfully in filthy
               prison clothes. He gazes around in wonder.*

BOLSHOV: Cor, this is a bit posh, isn't it?

LAZAR: We like it, father. It's good to see you, Samson.

LIPOCHKA: Hello daddy. Do sit down.

AGRAFENA: How could you do it, you silly old bear? How could you
               leave me alone and destitute, at my age?

BOLSHOV: Oh, shut it, woman. You've got Fominishna.

FOMINISHNA: Yes, you've got me! Now stop all this dreaful weeping and
               wailing. He isn't drunk or dead or anything.

AGRAFENA: He might as well be dead! He might as well be! Who
               would have thought that I would live to see my own
               husband locked up in gaol? Who?

LIPOCHKA: Come now, mother, there are lots of perfectly decent
               people doing time in prison, and some of them far
               superior to daddy.

BOLSHOV: Yes, there are. It's true. But prison's still prison. Can you
               imagine what it's like? No, daughter, I don't for one
               moment suppose you can. For forty years I've walked this
               town with dignity and self-respect. For forty years the
               good citizens have bowed their noses to the floor
               whenever they saw me coming. Now I go about with a
               soldier at my side. It's humiliating.

LAZAR: So – what's the situation with the creditors?

BOLSHOV: *(Delighted)* They will deal! They told me, 'We don't want
               to drag things out, whilst you decline in prison. Make us
               a serious proposition, and we'll call off the dogs.'

LAZAR: Well, you'd better give them what they want. Are they
               asking a lot?

BOLSHOV: Twenty-five kopecks per rouble.

LAZAR: That is a lot.

BOLSHOV: I know, but what can you say? They're businessmen. They won't settle for less. We'll have to give them the full twenty-five, like we offered them first time around.

LAZAR: How can we? You yourself said we couldn't possibly afford to pay more than ten. I understood my instructions. Haven't you been doing your mental arithmetic? Twenty-five kopecks per rouble comes to a devil of a lot of money! Samson, sit down, have a bite to eat. Get Fominishna to bring some vodka, mother. We'll all have a friendly drink and try and work this out.

AGRAFENA: What a good idea, Lazar. Fetch the vodka, Fominishna, if you please.

LAZAR: Twenty-five kopecks . . . well I don't know . . .

BOLSHOV: Look, I appreciate it's a lot, I can count. But if you'd spent six months rotting in a dungeon you'd be happy to pay the sods fifty. Every week I walk to that meeting with my escort, and every week they piss all over me, it's shameful.

AGRAFENA: Yes, it is.

Fominishna brings food and drink.

BOLSHOV: Thanks, Fominishna. Are they treating you well here?

FOMINISHNA: Every bit as well as you did, thank you.

AGRAFENA: Eat, husband, for the love of God. You look starved. What do they give you in there?

LAZAR: Please, eat as much as you can. Take all you want, we are frugal normally, but for you –

BOLSHOV: Thank you, Lazar, thank you.

AGRAFENA: O Lord, O Lord, what on earth can we do? Is this the will of God? O, what have we done, to be thus punished?

FOMINISHNA: We were born.

LIPOCHKA: Fominishna!

LAZAR: The Lord is merciful. You've often told me that. Somehow we'll get to the bottom of things. Though perhaps not just yet.

BOLSHOV: What's the solution, Lazar?

LAZAR: . . . If you're absolutely certain you want me to, I'll give them ten kopecks, as we agreed.

BOLSHOV: But where will I get the other fifteen? I can't make them out of lav paper, can I?

LAZAR: I really don't know what to suggest on that score.

BOLSHOV: Are you serious? What have you done with all the money?

LAZAR: See for yourself, sir. We've barely finished decorating the house. I'm starting a retail business. It's quite an outlay. Oh, come on, please, you haven't touched the food. Would you like a sherry? Mother, make him take something.

AGRAFENA: Eat, Samson. Eat! I'll pour you a sherry.

BOLSHOV: . . . Save me, children. Save me.

LAZAR: I actually find it mildly insulting that you should be asking me what I've done with the money, father. You know as much about business as I do. You know a large capital sum is required to get anything going. And your daughter had to have a decent place to live, didn't she? It's not as if I'm doing all this for my personal gain. And if you reside round here, you got to have the little extras, the ponies and that, or the neighbours – well you know.

It's your grandchildren I'm really thinking of, Samson,
in actual fact.

LIPOCHKA: Daddy, you can't ask this of us. We'd be left penniless.
We're not streetcorner traders, we're respectable people.

LAZAR: Think intelligently about it, please. Nothing's possible
nowadays without capital. Christ, without capital you can
scarcely make a living.

LIPOCHKA: Daddy, I lived with you till I was twenty years old, and
I never went out the front door. But I'm in society now!
You don't want to send me back to wearing nasty cotton
frocks, do you?

BOLSHOV: I can't believe I'm hearing this. I'm not asking for
charity. I'm asking for the return of my own property!
Are you human beings or what are you?

LIPOCHKA: Oh, we're human beings, daddy.

LAZAR: We would be only too delighted to pay your creditors,
father, if the sum they were asking was not so absurd.

BOLSHOV: I begged them to lower the rate. I got on my knees and
I begged. These are men who used to go in fear of me.

LIPOCHKA: We've already told you that ten kopecks is our absolute
limit. Any more is just unrealistic! But if you won't listen,
there's very little point in pursuing it further.

BOLSHOV: What you're saying, Lipochka, is 'Away you go to gaol,
you old fool. Away you go to debtors' gaol for the rest of
your life. Serves you right too.' Well, I hope it teaches you
a lesson. Be content with what you've got. Don't dream
of enormous fortunes – they disappear into thin air. If you
play for high stakes, one day you'll be stung rotten, you'll
end up throwing yourself in the Moscow River from the
great stone bridge. Then before you're dead they'll haul
you out with a hook through your tongue and sling you in
some awful prison.

They are silent. Bolshov drinks deep.

Yes, consider it. Consider what it's like, walking down
the road to the house of correction. It seems a hundred
miles long! It feels like the Lord pulling your tortured
soul through the slimier regions of hell. Judas sold Christ
for money, Lazar, and what happened to him?

FOMINISHNA: He got rich, didn't he?

BOLSHOV: Then once you're rotting in your cell there'll be the
lawyers, the investigations, the Courts of Commerce,
the Criminal Court . . . ! They are calling it malice
aforethought, you see. I may very well go to Siberia.
Won't you give me the money? I don't want to go to
Siberia!

LAZAR: You are making a song and dance of it, if I may say so,
Samson.

BOLSHOV: Money. I've got to have money. Nothing but money will
do.

LAZAR: Well . . . If you'll agree to leave us in peace . . . I'll go up
another five kopecks.

BOLSHOV: Twenty-five! I need twenty-five! After all these blasted
years! We had a gentleman's agreement!

LAZAR: It is rather a lot, that's the problem.

BOLSHOV: A nest of snakes. I despair of you. *(He curls up in a
pathetic heap on the floor.)*

Pause. Then Agrafena launches herself at Lazar.

AGRAFENA: You savage! You thief!

LAZAR: Get off me!

AGRAFENA: You're a thief in the night, you! You'll never have my
blessing. I hope you shrivel up one day while you're
counting your money, shrivel up and turn to sawdust.
Rotten, beastly savage! I damn you to hell!

LAZAR: Quiet! Do you think the Lord approves of language like that? The old man's not used to the drink, is he? He's hopelessly pissed.

LIPOCHKA: You do love damning people to hell, mother, don't you? She loves damning people to hell, Lazar. Though she's done more than enough to end up there herself. Which is probably why God didn't send her any more children.

AGRAFENA: He realised he'd punished me enough when he sent me you!

TISHKA: Mr. Bolshov, I'm afraid the guard has returned to take you back to prison.

LAZAR: Oh dear.

BOLSHOV: *(Rising)* I am leaving you, children. Farewell.

LAZAR: We'll figure it out, Samson.

BOLSHOV: We won't figure it out. The deal is off. Don't pay a single kopeck for me. Let them do their worst. Goodbye.

LAZAR: Goodbye, sir.

LIPOCHKA: Bye, daddy.

LAZAR: The Lord is merciful. It'll all turn out all right.

BOLSHOV: Goodbye, old girl.

AGRAFENA: Goodbye, Samson. Will they let me come to visit you?

BOLSHOV: I don't know.

AGRAFENA: If you go to Siberia you'll die.

BOLSHOV: Yes. Goodbye, daughter, little Lipochka. Well, now you're going to be rich and live alongside your betters, just like you always wanted. You'll go to society parties. You'll go to costume balls. And eventually you'll go to hell. But don't forget, Olimpiada, whilst you're out enjoying yourself, that somewhere there are prison cells, with iron bars, and prisoners sitting behind them.

Exit Bolshov, then Agrafena and Fominishna.

LAZAR: What a damned awkward business, Olimpiada. I do feel sorry for your father. Maybe I really ought to go and haggle with his creditors? My filial duty to my benefactor? What do you think?

LIPOCHKA: Do what you want, darling. Nothing to do with me.

LAZAR: Tishka!

TISHKA: Here boss.

LAZAR: Fetch a suitable coat for me to meet Bolshov's creditors in.

TISHKA: I know exactly the one. *(Exit)*

Rispolozhensky approaches.

RISPOLO: Hello? May I come in?

LIPOCHKA: Who's that?

LAZAR: It's Rispolozhensky.

LIPOCHKA: Ugh. If there's one thing I cannot stand it's a failure.

Enter Rispolozhensky.

RISPOLO: Is that vodka on the table? What a coincidence!

LAZAR: Don't tell me, your hands were just starting to shake.

RISPOLO: My dear Olimpiada, how marvellous it is to see you. What are you doing just at the moment?

LIPOCHKA: Leaving.

Exit Lipochka.

RISPOLO: *(Pours, drinks.)* Cheers, Lazar. First of the day.

LAZAR: Would you be civil enough to tell me why you're here, Rispolozhensky?

RISPOLO: *(Laughs)* You've got a sense of humour, Lazar, if nothing else. You know why!

LAZAR: I don't.

RISPOLO: For money, that's why. I've no idea what your other callers come for, but I come, as usual, for money.

LAZAR: I think you come much too often.

RISPOLO: That's because you only give me five roubles a time. I'm down on my luck. And I've a large family to support.

LAZAR: Well, you're not getting a hundred whenever you show your face.

RISPOLO: If you paid me in full what you owe me, there wouldn't be the need.

LAZAR: You arsehole. You're a walking disaster. Why should I give you money?

RISPOLO: You made me a promise.

LAZAR: I never. I'm so tired of this. You've taken your bribe, you did well out of it, that's your fucking lot.

RISPOLO: But I'm due fifteen hundred more!

LAZAR: Got it in writing, have you, Rispolozhensky? Anyway what's it supposed to be for – swindling Bolshov?

RISPOLO: Swindling Bolshov? I haven't swindled Bolshov. Good heavens, no! But I worked very hard on those contracts.

Please, Lazar – give me your promissory note if nothing else.

LAZAR: A promissory note? Not likely! I'd never see the back of you.

RISPOLO: You're taking the bread out of my children's mouths!

LAZAR: *(Gives money.)* Five roubles for bread.

RISPOLO: No, I'm not accepting that, I want my rightful due.

           Tishka enters. He carries Lazar's oldest, dirtiest coat. He helps Lazar out of his frock coat and into the old coat.

LAZAR: And how do you plan to go about getting it? Thanks, Tishka.

TISHKA: Don't want the creditors thinking you're a toff, do we, sir?

RISPOLO: What you have paid me has not bought my tongue.

LAZAR: That's all right, then, you can lick my boots.

RISPOLO: I am not licking your boots. I am going to speak out. There must be some right-minded people left in the world.

LAZAR: *(Surveys the audience.)* Sorry, no there ain't. At least, none who'll listen to you.

RISPOLO: They will! When I tell them about you. When I catalogue your iniquities. I'll accuse you in public, Lazar! I'll drag you through the courts!

LAZAR: The courts? You haven't got a prayer. You're as guilty as anyone.

RISPOLO: You wait and see! You wait and see!

LAZAR: . . . I'm waiting.

RISPOLO: *(Turns to the audience.)* Ladies and gentlemen – can I have the lights up please – ladies and gentlemen, this man –

LAZAR: Here, you can't do that.

TISHKA: *(To audience.)* He's so drunk he's not thinking straight.

RISPOLO: You shut your bleeding gob! – Ladies and gents I have a wife and five kids and great holes in my boots, look!

LAZAR: He's a compulsive liar, ladies and gentlemen. Not a responsible citizen at all. That's enough, Rispolozhensky, come and have a drink.

RISPOLO: No! No I won't!

LAZAR: You'll get yourself in trouble.

RISPOLO: He robbed his father-in-law, and now he's robbing me! I've got a wife and five kids and boots with holes in!

TISHKA: Why don't you get them re-soled?

RISPOLO: I'll have you sent to Siberia!

TISHKA: Oh yeah?

LAZAR: Please don't believe any of this silliness, ladies and gentlemen, it's all a pack of lies. This character is completely worthless. Ignore him. – You're pathetic, Rispolozhensky, you're a born loser. I wouldn't do business with you again in a million years. Look at yourself. You're a shambles. You're ridiculous.

RISPOLO: He stole everything he's got! He's a complete fucking bastard, ladies and gentlemen!

LAZAR: No I'm not!

RISPOLO: Yes you are! – Isn't he? He is, isn't he?

*Enter Agrafena, Bolshov, Fominishna, Ustinya, from
all sides. Lipochka enters and stands by her husband.*

AGRAFENA: He took my house and sold it! It was full of lovely things.

USTINYA: And he cheated *me*! A lady! The bugger robbed me blind!

LAZAR: My my, you have got a temper, haven't you, Ustinya?

FOMINISHNA: His brain is bathed in poison, ladies and gentlemen.

ALL: Yes, it is!

RISPOLO: He keeps my children hungry. He's worse than any of us.

LAZAR: I don't know what you're talking about. Are you having a
                nightmare, perhaps?

RISPOLO: No, Lazar, I'm just waking up!

AGRAFENA: Damn you, Lazar!

FOMINISHNA: You won't get away with it, Lazar.

BOLSHOV: One day your turn will come.

LAZAR: I nearly forgot to mention, ladies and gentlemen, whilst
                I have your ear – I'm about to open a department store.
                You'll all be hugely welcome. Quality goods. Incredible
                value for money.

LIPOCHKA: I love you, Lazar.

LAZAR: And I love you, my darling. *(They kiss.)* All right, we'll
                have those lights off now, shall we? Get back on the stage,
                you lot.

                A chorus of 'why?' and 'no!'

LIPOCHKA: Get back here and sing the song like you're supposed to!
                It's the end of the play! These good people don't go to the
                theatre to hear a lot of political nonsense. It's not
                fashionable any more.

Further refusals from the cast.

LAZAR: Play, Tishka.

              Tishka plays the accordion.

              Sing! Dance!

LIPOCHKA: Or don't you want to get paid . . . ?

              *Reluctantly the company return to the stage and perform
              the final number. Lazar and Lipochka yell at them to sing
              louder, dance faster. Eventually they seem to be satisfied.*

LAZAR &   *(Together)* Now that's what we call . . . family
LIPOCHKA: entertainment!

THE END

ANATOL

Arthur Schnitzler
Translated by Michael Robinson

Arthur Schnitzler's *Anatol* was written in the closing years
of the nineteenth century, as the over-ripe Austro-
Hungarian Empire hurtled towards the First World War
and the changes in sexual and social attitudes which
followed it. The writing is sharp, witty and fresh, and
presented here in a version which precisely captures the
elusive spirit of the original. Anatol rebounds from society
hostess to bareback rider, from actress to mondaine
fiancée, creating a kaleidoscopic impression of a new age.

'*Schnitzler's most amusing and original play*'
THE DAILY TELEGRAPH

'*. . . an unsparing masterpiece, far ahead of its time.*'
THE SUNDAY TELEGRAPH

'*Arthur Schnitzler's Anatol resembles a theatrical almanac*
for male lechers, which must have been calculated to dry
up the last gasps of sexual romanticism in fin de siècle
Vienna.'
THE GUARDIAN

'*Michael Robinson's crisp, new translation, as dry as a fine*
sparkling wine, lends a wonderful sense of irony to an
evening that fizzes with brittle wit and yet has a deeper
melancholy.'
PLAYS INTERNATIONAL

'*. . . it cries out to be given a major production.*'
THE LONDON DAILY NEWS

£4.50

ABSOLUTE CLASSICS – ABSOLUTE PRESS

THERESE RAQUIN

Emile Zola
Translated by Pip Broughton

Zola's own dramatisation of his famous novel is a taut psychological thriller, an intense story of adultery, murder and revenge, full of passion and obsession streaked with social satire. It is Zola's finest play which today retains its fascination for audiences and proved a great success in this translation by Pip Broughton, when it was premièred at the Liverpool Playhouse and later revived at the Warehouse Theatre, Croydon.

'A gripping yarn'
THE GUARDIAN

*'Pip Broughton's fine translation confirms this
as a mesmerising drama of obsessive crime and
passion committed in the stultifying ambience of the Paris
petit bourgeoisie.'*
TIME OUT

*'Zola's steamy story of a sexual passion that plumbs the
murky depths of murder, revenge and retribution'*
CITY LIMITS

£3.95

ABSOLUTE CLASSICS – ABSOLUTE PRESS

THUNDER IN THE AIR

August Strindberg
Translated by Eivor Martinus

August Strindberg's *Thunder In The Air* takes place in late
summer. The heat is oppressive, two elderly gentlemen
are planning a leisurely evening walk along the avenue,
the baker is jam-making, a young relative is busy around
the house, suddenly there is a rush of movement when a
young dishevelled woman appears. Old passions flare up
as balanced reason is toppled and the younger generation
is almost swept away by the emotional storm that ensues.
Thunder In The Air (1907) was the first of Strindberg's five
chamber plays, written when he had his own small
theatre in Stockholm. At the time of publication this play
has not been given a major production in Great Britain,
despite being regarded as one of the masterpieces of
world theatre.

*'It is a sulphurous, atmospheric work full of summer
lightning . . . why doesn't someone here prove August is for
the people?'*
THE GUARDIAN

August Strindberg (1849-1912) is perhaps best known for
his taut naturalistic dramas written during the break-up
of his first marriage. His latter plays, which are loosely
labelled 'symbolist' or 'expressionistic', have only recently
been appreciated outside of his native Sweden.

Eivor Martinus was born in Sweden but came to Britain in
her teens. She has since taken a degree in English and
Swedish literature and apart from publishing five original
novels, she has written two stage plays and translated
numerous works, notably the Strindberg premières
which were staged at the Gate Theatre in 1985.

£4.50

ABSOLUTE CLASSICS – ABSOLUTE PRESS

TURCARET

Alain René-Lesage
Translated and adapted by John Norman

Fraud, theft, extortion and sexual corruption: a society which sells off and farms out the power of taxation into private hands reaps its own harvest. Not a future nightmare but a classic eighteenth century French comedy. In the age when the Sun King's coffers were empty and the state machinery colluded with its tax gatherers to defraud itself, financiers made tremendous fortunes. Turcaret is one of these men – fingers in all monetary pies, legitimate and illegitimate, speculating wildly to increase his fortunes, loaning money at usurious rates, at the same time aspiring towards respectability through marriage and nobility. To such men a myriad of rogues attach themselves.

'Turcaret is generally accepted as one of the best of French comedies, few people in this country can ever have seen it . . . an unjustly neglected foreign classic.'
THE SUNDAY TELEGRAPH

'. . . a real discovery . . . the play is sharp and brisk, and might have been written jointly by Molière and Goldsmith . . .'
THE SUNDAY TIMES

'a biting social satire . . . this is the "Serious Money" of its day . . .'
THE GUARDIAN

'. . . it is a fascinating cynical comedy . . . John Norman's adaptation is full of twentieth century colloquialisms and the piece would probably work well in modern dress . . . The National Theatre . . . should now consider staging the play itself.'
THE DAILY TELEGRAPH

£4.50

ABSOLUTE CLASSICS – ABSOLUTE PRESS

PAINS OF YOUTH

Ferdinand Bruckner
Translated by Daphne Moore

Pains of Youth, written in 1926, was the play that
established Ferdinand Bruckner. It is the sort of play that
is written once in every generation, voicing the frustr-
ation and disillusionment of youth in a world that is
hopelessly out of joint.

The play depicts with unprecendented candour the
moral corruption and cycnicism of a group of medical
students. For these young people, youth itself is a fatal
disease and the idea of death by suicide is always present in
their minds.

'Discovery of the Year . . .'
THE GUARDIAN.

'Pains of Youth speaks urgently for today'
THE LISTENER

*'The ebullient translation of a play that has knocked me
for six is by Daphne Moore'*
THE FINANCIAL TIMES

*'The play is a remarkable find . . . it follows logically after
Schnitzler . . . and with its Mephistophelean darkness and
vampire-like conclusion it evokes Strindberg and Pinter'.*
THE LONDON DAILY NEWS

£4.50

ABSOLUTE CLASSICS – ABSOLUTE PRESS